THE PRISONER PEAR

stories

from

the

lake

THE PRISONER PEAR

by Elissa Minor Rust

Swallow Press / Ohio University Press

Athens

Swallow Press / Ohio University Press, Athens, Ohio 45701
www.ohio.edu/oupress

Swallow Press / Ohio University Press books
are printed on acid-free paper ⊗ ™

14 13 12 11 10 09 08 07 06 05 5 4 3 2 1

Jacket/cover and title page spread: *Three Pears and a Plumb*
(detail) by Dan J. Annarino

Library of Congress Cataloging-in-Publication Data
Rust, Elissa Minor, 1977–
    The prisoner pear : stories from the lake / by Elissa Minor Rust.
      p. cm.
    ISBN 0-8040-1083-8 (cloth : alk. paper) — ISBN 0-8040-1078-1
(pbk. : alk. paper)
    1. Lake Oswego (Or.)—Fiction. 2. Crime—Fiction. I. Title.
    PS3618.U775P75 2005
    813'.6—dc22
                                                                    2005018721

For Christopher

Contents

Acknowledgments

Some of these stories first appeared in magazines: "Vital Organs" in *Carve Magazine*, "Iris and Megan Imagine Alternatives" in *Orchid: A Literary Review*, and "The Weight of Bones" in *The Baltimore Review*. The author also gratefully acknowledges Literary Arts, Inc., for a fellowship that made a tremendous difference toward the completion of this book.

For their guidance, assistance, and friendship, the author would like to thank the following people: Nancy Minor, Warden Minor, Melissa Pritchard, Jay Boyer, Ron Carlson, Marjorie Sandor, Quinn Minor, J. Minor, Gina Clark, Elaina Asay, Rob Sunderlage, Pat Rust, Harold Rust, Nancy Basmajian, and David Sanders. Special thanks to Shannon Castleton and Lynn Sokei, whose friendship and encouragement on early drafts are beyond words. And, finally, thanks to Chloë and Elias, the most amazing distractions a writer could ask for.

I

Downtown/First Addition

The Prisoner Pear

A resident of Oswego Pointe reported the
mysterious draining of his fish tank. He found
no puddle, no signs of a forced entry, and his
fish scattered around the bottom of the tank.

—Lake Oswego Review police blotter

THE FIRST THING was the spontaneous death of his houseplants. When Jordan left his apartment at ten on a Saturday morning, all three of them were alive and well. The philodendron on
top of the television, the strange grassy-looking one with varie-
gated leaves, the African violet in the windowsill. By the time he
returned home from his lunch out, they were all wilted and dry,
brown from root to tip.

He had asked for a miracle, a sign. In its place, he got dead
plants.

The lunch: his girlfriend, Miranda, met him at Manzana wearing a long sweeping skirt, nervously brushing her hair from her face
while they waited for her parents to arrive. A friend had dropped
her off. Her parents were twenty minutes late, which Miranda
said was probably to assert control, and the four were seated on

the far end of the restaurant, opposite the bar, although Miranda's mother ordered three brandies before the check came. And then Jordan kissed Miranda's mother on the cheek, shook hands with her father, and he and Miranda watched them drive off in the black Mercedes whose license plate read MYBENZ, disappearing ever deeper into the depths of Lake Oswego.

They walked back to Jordan's place, past the fountain where swimsuit-clad children played, past the upscale antique shop on the corner, into the crosswalk, and down into the Oswego Pointe apartments, where he found his houseplants withered and dry. It was, he thought, a very bad sign. Miranda didn't seem to notice.

* * *

He had purchased a ring. Over the telephone, his older sister had told him the etiquette was to spend two months of his salary on an engagement ring. Two months of his salary as a manager at the UPS store would buy Miranda a simple but elegant diamond, according to the salesman at the Shane Company, and he picked out a solitaire in white gold, the diamond shaped like a very miniature pear.

That was three weeks ago. Since then, he had kept it inside an old shoe box in the closet and tried to work up the courage to give it to her. It was harder than he'd thought, which he took as a sign that maybe Miranda wasn't the one. Sometimes, when Miranda wasn't there, he would pull the box from the closet, open the lid, and imagine the ring on her finger. He imagined her wearing it with her black dress that hit just below the knee, he imagined her wearing it with nothing on at all while they made love here, in his apartment, he imagined her wearing it years from now, children hanging from her hip, his wife. She looked spectacular in all his imaginings, which he took as a sign that maybe this was it.

Jordan and Miranda didn't discuss the lunch with her parents for most of the afternoon. Jordan lined up his dead houseplants on the balcony and drowned them with water from the kitchen sink, hoping some sunlight and nourishment would bring them back to life, and Miranda fed the fish in the tank along the wall of the living room. Then they sat on his couch, Miranda's feet in his lap, and watched television until they were both hungry for dinner. When Miranda's phone rang, she dug it from her purse, plugged her other ear, and paced the white linoleum in the kitchen. From what Jordan heard, Miranda told her mother that no, in fact, she wasn't coming home for dinner, she'd probably get a pizza with Jordan, and she didn't know when she'd be home.

Jordan asked her, Why haven't your parents ever invited me for dinner?

Miranda shrugged.

He asked, Why didn't your father even look at me today at lunch?

Miranda shrugged again. Listen, hon, she said. They have issues.

But Jordan knew what the issues were. Wasn't it an old story? Miranda's father wanted her with a stock analyst, a doctor, a software guru, even, not a twenty-six-year-old UPS store manager who didn't quite complete his last year of college. Miranda's father wanted her with a man whose family lived on the lake, like they did, a family they could invite over for cocktails and make business deals with, not a guy with hardly any roots from Roseberg, the armpit of Oregon.

Miranda sat on his lap and ran her bare foot teasingly up his leg, tickled his earlobe with little flicks of her tongue.

She said, Think I can convince you to order me a pizza?

* * *

Jordan, who wasn't really sure if he believed in God, had prayed: Just one little sign, please, so that I know I am doing the right thing. I love the girl. I think. That's enough, right? It doesn't have to be something big. Nothing showy—loaves, fishes, the whole nine yards. Just so long as I get it.

He thought, I am not doing this right.

Um, Amen.

* * *

Jordan's sister liked to tell him that he was painfully traditional when it came to romance.

When Jordan met the woman who would be his wife, he used to think, he would know it instantly. It was crazy, sure. He knew this. But he was convinced there would be a certain glow about her, that her hair (blond, probably) would sparkle, that they would lock eyes, etc. He used to imagine them in a short but intense courtship, then married in a small church wedding, white dress, their families in the front pews, the works. He thought about making love to her on their wedding night—not that they hadn't made love before, necessarily, but he never imagined making love to her until she was, well, his wife.

When Jordan met Miranda, she was mailing a birthday gift to an old college roommate. She walked through the door of the UPS store two weeks after he'd been transferred there from the Roseburg store. She had a brown leather handbag on her shoulder and her auburn hair swept up into a deliberately messy bun. He thought of what he'd been told about this town, how people had laughed when he told them where he was going and called it Lake Ego.

Jordan thought: Here is another Lake Oswego rich girl, shipping things to other parts of the world.

She was not particularly attractive, though he thought she had a nice smile. They hardly spoke while he weighed and metered her package, and then after she paid he watched her leave through the glass door, pushing the button on her key chain until the silver, shiny SUV she had driven beeped in response.

Jordan thought, and he would later hate that he thought this: She is not much to look at, but she has a great ass.

No instant attraction, no glow in the shape of a halo around her head.

It was Miranda who recognized him, not the other way around, when they ran into each other the next day at Noah's Bagels, and then again the following week in the pharmacy of the Albertsons.

Months later, when they first slept together, he thought, This is what it's like to sleep with a rich girl. They fell asleep on his sofa, and when they woke hours later, she scrambled for her clothes and wiped the sleep from her eyes, her hair matted against her face. He pulled her close after she pulled her shirt on, and tucked her against his body on the couch again for one last moment before she left. He was surprised how well she fit there, curved like a comma into the empty space against his body, and realized that she was just like any other girl, and that he'd grown accustomed to the smell of her.

Jordan thought: This is not how I'd expected it.

* * *

The second sign came on Monday. Jordan was leaning behind the counter at the store just after opening up. He saw a woman driving a Volvo pull into the parking space just in front of the store, and he watched her through the glare of the window as she unloaded four large grocery sacks and set them one by one on the curb. She was an older woman, but from what he could see through the glare of the glass, he thought she was attractive—her hair sleek and blond, her body perfectly shaped, the kind of firm, curvy body he imagined artists liked to sculpt. It wasn't until she came through the door, the sacks resting precariously in the curves of her arms, that he recognized her as Miranda's mother.

Jordan ran to the door and took the grocery sacks from her, uttering an awkward hello. He couldn't understand why he hadn't recognized her, although this was the first time he'd seen her without her husband or daughter. He carried the bags to the counter, then turned and smiled.

I take it you want to mail these? He asked. He looked inside for the first time and saw that they were filled with fruit.

Pears, she said. I'm sending them to my sister. She smiled at him as if what she'd just said was the most impressive thing he could have heard. A full year at the UPS store, and never had Jordan helped anyone ship fruit, let alone fruit in the same shape as the diamond in his shoe box. She said, How can I pack these so they'll make it all right? Jordan thought: My God, she has the fullest lips I've ever seen.

Jordan donned his knowing face, as if he mailed fruit all the time and knew just what to do. They reached into the bags and pulled the pears out one by one, placing them on the counter. Soon dozens of green anjou pears, not quite ripe, were staring him in the face. Next, they transferred the fruit into boxes divided into segments, placing each on a little bed of packing peanuts. When the boxes were filled, Jordan topped them off with shredded paper and sealed them shut.

Did you grow these yourself? he asked, suddenly conscious of how dumb he sounded, of how mediocre he must look in his tan uniform, his name badge crooked against his breast pocket. Miranda's mother nodded and said she had three large pear trees in her yard, just along the shoreline.

She said, They're the perfect fruit. Jordan raised his eyebrows in interest.

She said, The shape. Fits perfectly in your hand. Like this. She handed him a pear, told him he could keep it. And not only did it seem to fit there, it seemed to burn into his palm. He shifted his weight to his other foot and thanked her.

As she picked up her purse to leave, Jordan assured her that within a day her pears would be in the air, making their way toward her sister's home in Connecticut.

He fell asleep that night with the pear on his nightstand and the vision of those perfectly boxed pieces of fruit, resting on white Styrofoam, their small brown stems staring up at him like eyes. The pillow next to him smelled like Miranda, and he wished she were here now. He fell asleep and dreamed of her covered in pears, her lips suddenly as round and full as her mother's, her body as firm. He dreamed about boxes and boxes of pear-shaped diamonds, somewhere in the air, making their way to Connecticut.

He woke finally convinced he would give her that ring. But by the time he'd finished his breakfast, fed the fish, and poured more water onto the still-dead plants on his balcony, he was acutely aware of how different this life would be from the one she was used to, and he wasn't so sure anymore.

* * *

Before he even left for work, Miranda called Jordan to say that her parents had invited him to dinner that night. He didn't think to ask whether Miranda had talked them into the invitation or they'd come to it on their own—he liked to think, actually, that it was

Miranda's mother's idea, that their encounter at the UPS store had left her more interested in getting to know the man dating her daughter.

He assigned one of the younger employees to lock up for him so he could leave early and pick up something nice to take with him to dinner that night—a bottle of wine, maybe, or an unusual-looking dessert. He walked up the street to the gourmet foods store, thankful that for once it wasn't raining. Once inside, he felt awkward and out of place, certain every person in the store—customers and employees alike—was staring at his brown UPS uniform as a sure symbol that he didn't fit in. He walked the aisles, seeing only things he was certain weren't right: white chocolate-covered cherries, logs of black licorice with apricot fondant centers, chocolate pound cakes covered in a fine dusting of ground almonds and wrapped in clear plastic with a gold-tinted bow, row after row of wines with identical-looking labels.

He thought of Miranda's mother, the way her blond hair swept the tops of her shoulders when she moved her head. He thought of her assured manner, the striking fullness of her lips, natural or no.

He thought of her sipping one brandy after another the afternoon he and Miranda had lunched with her parents at Manzana. He remembered thinking it was an odd choice, a masculine drink, if such a thing was possible.

The wine steward showed him their choices in brandy. Most of them involved fruit—raspberry brandy, orange brandy, a brandy whose label promised a hint of red plum. And then he saw it: there, the last bottle on the aisle, a bottle of brandy with a full-grown pear inside. The bottle itself seemed pear-shaped, the smooth lines and curves of the glass following the outline of the pear almost exactly. Jordan imagined a worker on an assembly line in some

French province trying to stuff that enormous pear through the bottle's small neck. Impossible.

How do they get that thing in there? He asked the steward, who was beginning to look annoyed.

Grows that way, he answered. They strap the bottle to the trees in the spring, before the fruit forms.

How could he resist? Jordan spent fifty dollars on the brandy, more than he'd ever spent on twelve ounces of liquid in his life. He carried it home carefully and placed it on his nightstand while he showered, next to Miranda's mother's pear. He thought about it while the water ran down his face, how it was almost criminal to subject a living organism to such a fate before it had grown into itself. To come into your own but be surrounded by glass. A prisoner of somebody else's whim.

He stepped out of the shower and toweled himself off. In his bedroom, before dressing, he stood in front of the mirror. He liked what he saw, always had—just the right amount of hair on his chest, a fairly flat stomach, good muscle tone. And then he thought of the brandy again, and felt a jolt of fear run through him and settle in the empty space above his stomach, just behind his better-than-average abs.

My God, he thought. He'd prayed for a sign—this was as good a sign as any. How literally should he take this?

I am the pear, he thought.

* * *

When Miranda arrived at Jordan's apartment to pick him up for dinner, he was nervously tugging at the collar of his shirt, which he'd put on with a nice pair of jeans. He'd wondered if Miranda would want him to change his clothes or give him last-minute tips, but she didn't even look at what he was wearing when she came through the door. She gave him a long kiss, said, You ready? and took his hand as they walked to the car. Jordan was slightly annoyed. She was acting as if they were meeting friends for pizza and a movie, as if this were any regular night out together. She hadn't even asked what it was he carried under his arm, where he'd pressed the pear-shaped bottle.

But Miranda's mother seemed thrilled. I've seen these, she said. And then: How fun! And then when Miranda wasn't looking, her mother gave him a more poignant stare, and then smiled. He wondered what, if anything, he should read into it.

The dinner: they ate on her parents' back deck, overlooking the boat dock below them and a wide expanse of the lake. During moments of long silences, Jordan watched the geese on the dock sunning themselves and looking upward in their direction, hopeful for scraps. Jordan wished he could throw them something. When they were done eating and they had each had a share of the brandy, Miranda and her mother cleared the plates, insisting the men sit, and went inside to do the dishes. Watching them disappear through the sliding glass door, Miranda winking at him, Jordan imagined for a brief moment he was part of this life. He imagined that he and Miranda's father were about to talk business, or smoke after-dinner cigars, while their women folk cleaned up, all ordinary as pie. Jordan knew he had been given the perfect opportunity to ask Miranda's father for her hand, a tradition he had always planned to follow when he found the woman he wanted to marry. But the words seemed to stick somewhere in the base of his throat, and he couldn't get them out. This, he thought, is not a very good sign.

Miranda's father said, How are things at the UPS store?

Jordan looked across the water, at the massive houses rising from the shore on the other side. He said, I'm hoping to buy a few stores of my own someday, and then felt like an idiot for having said it. Miranda's father looked surprised, then nodded, and ran a toothpick along his gum line.

Jordan thought: But is it so far-fetched? Maybe I am planning to buy some stores. And then he felt bigger, better, because suddenly, he had a plan.

Miranda and her mother reemerged onto the deck, her mother carrying a pair of binoculars. Miranda said, My mom wants to show you her birds, and she motioned for him to stand at the deck railing. Her mother told him about a pair of bald eagles, the only two in Lake Oswego or anywhere else that she knew of, for that matter, nesting in the giant fir tree next to their deck. She handed him the binoculars and he looked through them, scanning the now magnified needles for any sign of a nest, for little bird shapes. Then he noticed how much bigger the houses looked across the lake now, how he could practically see inside them, all their trimmings exposed.

Jordan handed the binoculars to Miranda's mother and apologized.

Maybe next time, she said. When she pulled the binoculars in against her chest, Jordan noticed for the first time the ring on her left hand. It spanned practically from one knuckle to the next, two carats at least, shaped like a perfect pear. His heart sank.

Miranda excused them and told Jordan she'd like to take him out on the boat. They walked to the dock, the geese scattering, and Miranda started the engine as they pushed away. He watched the things of her house grow smaller as they headed farther out in the water: the deck, the white lights illuminated along the railing, her parents like statues, staring after them. The pear trees along the shoreline, whose branches he knew only days before had hung low with voluptuous ripe fruit.

Miranda steered the boat down the middle of the lake, pointing out the houses whose occupants she knew, any gossip she could share about them. They rode past the rear of the movie theater, the lakeside hotels, making a violent V-shaped wake behind them as they went. It was strange to Jordan, seeing the lake this way. He'd only seen it from the street, what glimpses he could catch of it between the houses and the trees. And now here he was, in the center of it. It was like seeing the town from the inside out, as if the lake were its heart and the rest (the Lake Oswego he knew) merely its bones and skin. Being there on the inside, he realized that unlike most men his age, he'd never much aspired to this sort of wealth, to a house on the lake, a boat of his own. But here, in the heart of it, for the first time he saw it as a club he'd actually like to join, a way of life he could get used to. The sun had begun to set and the houses receded farther against the trees and the shore as darkness settled in, their lighted windows popping out like watchful eyes.

Miranda slowed the motor and steered the boat farther away from the orange buoys, along a shoreline peppered only with trees and meticulously manicured lawns. They were in a small private cove, out of sight from the houses, the theaters, the hotels. Miranda turned to him.

She said, Have you ever made love in a boat?

Jordan smiled. Never on a Tuesday, he answered, but he didn't move toward her. He could think only about the fact that the more he was around her mother, the less appealing Miranda looked— more childlike, bland. He looked at his watch, and soon Miranda revved up the motor again, and they found themselves quickly approaching her mother's pear trees, the geese scattering again to allow them ashore.

Jordan thought: I would be marrying all this. As she climbed out of the boat and brushed the dust from her skirt, Jordan found it was not altogether unthinkable that Miranda could one day carry herself with the same sexy assurance as her mother's. A man could hope.

Jordan thought: I am the pear.

* * *

Jordan's sister thought a proposal should be traditional and romantic. Dinner at a fine restaurant, violin music, cheesecake for dessert, the ring in the pocket of his slacks. He could kneel on one knee, if he felt so moved, though that wasn't, she thought, entirely necessary.

Jordan's friend from college had rented the planetarium at the Oregon Museum of Science and Industry to propose to his girlfriend. He brought his guitar, serenaded her while the stars danced and pirouetted overhead. Then he pulled out the ring, the "biggest star of all," and asked her to be his wife.

The college kid who was working for the summer at Noah's Bagels (where Jordan always took his lunch) was convinced that women liked very large, very public proposals. Over the loudspeaker at the airport, say, or on the scoreboard at a Blazers game.

Jordan's mother had once said that the best marriage proposals were spontaneous and unplanned, something that catches both parties completely by surprise.

Jordan had no idea.

* * *

As Miranda drove Jordan home from her parents' house, Jordan found himself quiet and withdrawn. He thought: was the night a success or a failure? And the fact that he couldn't quite decide distressed him. His seat began to feel warm, and he saw that Miranda had turned on his seat warmer for him. At his feet was the pear-shaped bottle, now drained of its liquor, the pear lying spent and ragged at the bottom. He couldn't quite explain it, but just before they left, hoping Miranda's parents wouldn't notice, he'd grabbed the bottle and tucked it inside his jacket.

He held the bottle in place with his foot to keep it from rolling. The inside of Miranda's car was meticulously clean, as always, the gray leather seats and dash as pristine as if nobody had ever touched them or sat on them. He marveled at the bells and whistles of her car as if seeing them for the first time—the digital thermometer that told her what temperature it was under her tires at any given second (sixty-five degrees right now), the five-disk compact disk changer, so many stereo and climate controls that it would take years to learn what to do with them. When they'd first started dating, he'd been embarrassed by the old Civic sitting up on blocks in the garage he'd rented at Oswego Pointe, out of commission for over nine months now, but he'd begun to feel comfortable in the front seat of her car, think of it as his own, even.

He looked at Miranda, stone-faced behind the steering wheel, and wished he'd moved toward her in the boat earlier. He wanted to ask her if *she* had ever made love in a boat, but he was afraid of the answer. He thought of a teenage Miranda, out on the boat after a high school dance, a future Yale boy fumbling with the buttons on her cashmere sweater, the hooks on the back of her strapless taffeta gown. He pictured an older Miranda with her ex-boyfriend (the son of her father's friend) making love on that boat, like a scene from a bad Hollywood movie: music playing from an unknown source, fish leaping into the air around them, a pair of bald eagles circling overhead. And then, of course, the unthinkable: Miranda's mother and father on that boat, or Miranda's mother alone, or Miranda's mother with another man—but no. He shook his head to rid himself of the thought.

When they reached Oswego Pointe, Miranda parked the car and they held hands as they made their way along the walkway to his apartment. Jordan unlocked the door and stared into the dark front room, feeling along the wall for the light switch. When he popped it upward, nothing happened, and he silently cursed under his breath. It was the second time in a week the power had gone out.

He said, Power's out, and guided Miranda inside gently with his hand on the inward curve of her back. They stood in the front room for a moment and let their eyes adjust to the dark. Soon, Jordan began to make out shapes: the sweeping curve of the sofa's arm, the table to the right of the door, the breakfast bar that separated kitchen from living room. He worked his way slowly into the kitchen and searched through the junk drawer until he found an old flashlight. He turned it on and stood it upright on the counter, its light concentrated on the ceiling but bleeding outward enough that he could see to reach into the fridge and remove two soda cans. He stopped when he heard Miranda gasp.

Jordan, she said.

He turned and looked at her. The eerie glow from the flashlight surrounded her human shape like an aura, a full-bodied halo. She was staring at the living room wall, in the direction of the fish tank. Jordan walked over to her and she pointed at the tank: Jordan, she said, look.

He squinted his eyes and saw that the tank had been entirely drained of its water. It was empty except for a thin layer of rocks along the bottom, the green plastic plants sitting atop them as if nothing out of the ordinary had happened. The fish were there, too, lying on that bed of rocks, their skin dry, their eyes staring straight at him with a deep, silver glow. It was a knowing look they gave him, and Jordan had to look above the fish, at the empty glass, because of it. He walked over to the tank and felt the carpet underneath for wetness, but his hand hit only plain, dry, carpet. There was no water to be found.

He looked at Miranda, her skin glowing in the flashlight beam like a promise, then back at the fish. Nobody moved. He had been waiting for an unmistakable sign, and here, strange though it was, was his answer. He thought he had been afraid of becoming a prisoner like that pear, but hadn't these fish met a worse fate? To feel like you had all the room you need to move and breathe, and yet to suddenly, inexplicably suffocate?

And it was just like that—thinking of the pear-shaped diamond in his closet, thinking of the dead houseplants, the boxes of pears being flown to Connecticut, the houses sitting on the lake like living, breathing organisms—that he knew what he wanted. Marriage was, after all, a package deal.

He would ask her to marry him. Tonight. Minutes from now, even.

But first, he wanted to taste the pear. He grabbed the bottle from where it stood on the counter and carried it to the empty tank. In one swift motion, he swung it toward the dead fish, sending small beams of glass flying in the dim light.

Miranda jumped, but didn't say a word. Jordan was conscious of her breathing, of her eyes on his figure outlined in the dark as he fished through the broken glass to find the pear, still heavy and wet with liquor. He brought it to his lips and bit into it unromantically, like a person would an apple, and only then noticed the trail of blood running down his index finger.

The pear tasted like brandy. That's all. Had he been blindfolded and fed this fruit, he would not have known it was a pear at all. Even worse than the disappointing flavor was the pear's texture: it folded under his tongue like mush.

Jordan held his bloody finger in the air and offered Miranda a bite of the pear. She laughed at him then and shook her head. They stood there like that for what seemed like an eternity—Jordan, the fish, Miranda, a perfect triangle in the semidarkness—while Jordan held his breath.

Iris and Megan

Imagine Alternatives

Two women standing on the corner of State
and A late at night were reported as possible
prostitutes by a delivery driver. The women
were not "working," but were waiting for a
cab ride home.

—*Lake Oswego Review* police blotter

Food Was the Taunting Nag

WHEN MEGAN AND Iris first met at the Ellentower Clinic
for Disordered Eating, they weighed one hundred and seventy-nine
pounds together. Megan first thought of the idea. She had been in
for a week when the grumpy nurse—the one with spiky black
hair and three earrings on each side—had her undress and step
on the scale. The nurse shook her head and told Megan she was
still at only eighty-four pounds. Later that day, Iris was admitted
to the inpatient program and Megan took a liking to her immediately. Big numbers, she told the newcomer, make them happy here.
So she linked arms with Iris after group therapy, added Iris's ninety-
five pounds to her own, and said, One hundred and seventy-nine:
now we are one.

Now they were one. And there *were* striking similarities. Both girls lived in Lake Oswego, within ten miles of each other. Both of their fathers were dentists. Megan was on the dance team at Lake Oswego High School, and Iris was a cheerleader at Lakeridge. They both had blond highlights in their hair, though Iris would readily admit that Megan's looked more natural. Neither one had kissed a boy, and they both wondered what it was like: was it merely a wet, sloppy encounter, or an opening up of something deep and hidden, an intimation of things to come?

And then.

For each of them, food was that taunting nag that would not relent. It was all the same: cherry pie, spinach quiche, scrambled eggs with salsa, cheese puffs, rocky road ice cream. Food was the unthinkable they couldn't get off their minds, the craving they couldn't get past their lips.

Sometimes, in their separate rooms, after their parents had left, Megan and Iris would lie in the dark, thinking what neither would admit to the other: If we are one, why not get our pounds down together, a perfect one-hundred-and-twenty-pound being, beautiful beyond all beautiful?

Army Fatigues and the Homecoming Dance

At group therapy their third week together, Dr. Leincroft said, Talk about the first time you remember feeling like food was the enemy. The way he said it made Megan think of a pork chop wearing army fatigues and chasing after her, a corn chip wielding a hand grenade and chucking it toward her mouth. She smiled at Iris, who giggled in response, as if she'd had the same vision.

Everyone in group had to answer.

For Iris, it was after the Homecoming dance, walking past the vending machines in the high school hallway and realizing she hadn't eaten all day. I felt proud, she said. I saw the other students buying pop and chips and thought how disgusting they all were.

Megan said, I honestly have no idea. But she thought about the late afternoons, after she'd gotten home from school, when she would disappear into her mother's walk-in closet and breathe in the scent of the cedar lining. She thought about the way she'd try everything on—her mom's high-heeled shoes, her nicest black gown, the one she wore to charity auctions. She'd drape her mother's scarves over her shoulder and cinch the belts on her mother's pants so she could see what her waistline looked like in the full-length mirror on the back of the closet door. And she'd look at the image reflected there and admire herself, then quickly feel mostly hate—for the heavy feeling in her stomach, for the warmth of her body behind all those clothes.

Megan and Iris thought, Is food the enemy?

What Iris Wore

When Iris was admitted to the clinic, she wore a short-sleeved green tee shirt over a long-sleeved white one, both from The Gap. She wore a pair of baggy blue jeans with no belt, frayed at the hem. She wore a pair of ankle weights under her jeans, to trick her parents into thinking she hadn't lost as much weight as they feared. She wore a pair of rubber Old Navy flip-flops, despite the classic November Oregon rain, and small silver braided rings on two of her toes. Her toenails were painted Kiss of Coral Pink. Iris had in her mind the image of a dancer she'd seen on a Gap commercial —a girl who looked no older than herself, moving in time behind Madonna—who had calves the size of a little boy's and perfect, pin-straight hair that hit her face just right when she bobbed her head.

When Iris was admitted to the clinic, she was the textbook case for her disease. Her heart was pumping in irregular patterns, speeding up at times, skipping beats at others. Sometimes she could hear it if she listened closely: thump thump, thump thump, long pause, thump. Iris hadn't had a period in four months. When she told Megan, she said, How awesome is that?

When Iris was admitted to the clinic, she could spend hours each day planning the perfect meal from recipes she'd memorized in her mother's cookbooks and magazines. Her dream meal: Dijon Chicken with Panko Crust (*Sunset Magazine*), Orzo with Peas and Mint (*Martha Stewart Living*), Zesty Carrots in Horseradish Sauce (*The Easy Vegetarian*), and for dessert, Double-Decker Chocolate Cake with Raspberry Puree and Powdered Sugar (her own invention).

When Iris was admitted, she knew she was grotesquely overweight, fat to the point that mirrors sickened her. She'd been spending hours Saturday mornings on the treadmill at Club Sport, where her parents were members, reading magazines aimed at middle-aged women. She loved the diet tips in *Woman's Day*, the articles on low-fat healthy eating in *Cosmopolitan*. She stopped eating red meat, then chicken, then anything containing fat, then most foods altogether. She watched her body shed its pounds over the last six months, relished each lower number on the scale.

And yet.

The Iris she saw in the mirror unremittingly reflected her flaws.

Megan and Iris Window Shop

Megan got her driver's license four months after she had been released from the clinic. She drove to Iris's house and picked her up for group therapy twice a week. What fantastic freedom! On one of the first sunny days of March, weighing two hundred and ten together, they skipped therapy at the last minute and drove into downtown Portland. Megan was too scared to parallel park, so they each chipped in for a parking garage.

Don't we feel like normal girls? Megan said. They walked along Salmon with their arms linked. Iris didn't say it, but she felt scared of the people they passed: a large man sitting on the cement with his belly hanging out of his shirt, a petite woman and a girl with thick hips waiting together under the bus stop shelter, a six-foot-tall businessman, thin as an Abercrombie model, walking briskly with a little silver phone to his left ear. The girls strolled the length of Meier and Frank and made comments about the headless mannequins, dolled up in the new spring lines. They used to think the models were beyond-belief-skinny, once-upon-a-dream-skinny, but if Megan and Iris had learned anything in the last year, it was that maybe, just maybe, that shape isn't quite so impossible. In one window, a mannequin wore a black halter top with a khaki miniskirt, in the next, layered tank tops and fitted cotton capris.

That's cute, Iris said, pointing to another.

Which?

That one, there, she said. The peach tank with spaghetti straps.

Megan said, Figures we'd be drawn to the clothing named after food. They giggled. A pair of boys walked by and whistled, so they pretended not to hear, acted casual.

In unison, they think: If only we had the bodies to pull off these clothes.

By the time they got home, Dr. Leincroft had called their parents. That night, from opposite sides of Oswego Lake, they sat at their computers to send each other instant messages.

Megan typed, R U OK?

Iris: They grounded me. Mom got ballistic and says she'll start weighing my food again.

Megan: Mine said ruin your own damn life.

Megan used the colon and parenthesis keys to type a sideways happy face, to show that she really didn't care.

The Tissue, in a Million Pieces

While they were still in the clinic, Megan told Iris about her family therapy. About the way her father sat in the padded chair with his legs crossed, pumping his top leg like a woman. About the way he nibbled at the tips and sides of his fingernails. About how his answer to everything was, I don't understand why she can't just start eating and get over it.

Megan told Iris about her family therapy: My little sister sits there with the snottiest look on her face, like she's all *See how you ruined my life* and *Why am I being punished for this?* Once she even said *Meg wants everyone to be sad for her, and now you are, aren't you?* And then—this was so cool!—the therapist was like *Sarah, having an older sister with an eating disorder makes you at risk too.* Sarah rolled her eyes like she's all that.

Megan told Iris: Mom sits there with a tissue wadded up in her hand. Like she needs to prevent eye makeup runnage at all times. By the end of the session, the tissue is in a million pieces, wet to shreds. She's like a freaking faucet. And then my dad's all *We're going to be fine, honey*, and pats all our backs and smiles at the therapist. I mean, God! He wears a tie to every session. A freaking tie.

Iris said, My dad wears a tie every time, too. She said, Must be a dentist thing.

Megan thought, but didn't say, Shit—could Sarah really end up like me?

Cancer and the Common Cold

Iris's mom started dropping the girls off at therapy again, a punishment both sets of parents came up with together. When group began, Dr. Leincroft said, Megan and Iris, we missed you last time, and some of the other girls nodded. Dr. Leincroft said, Today we're going to imagine alternatives.

Iris said, I wish I had cancer instead of anorexia.

Dr. Leincroft shifted in his seat and said, Why?

People feel sorry for you when you have cancer, she said. They write articles about you in the school paper and your friends shave their heads to show their support after chemo. I saw a group of kids do that on Oprah, she said.

Dr. Leincroft said, You don't think people feel sorry for you now? He blew his nose into a handkerchief.

One of the girls said, Hell no.

Another said, Don't they?

Iris said, It's in a different way. Iris started thinking about the smiles she got from teachers, the looks she got from the other students in the halls when she passed. The way nobody wanted to speak out loud where she'd been, or why. But they'd been so quick to admire her months before—Iris, you are so skinny! I wish I was that skinny! You look so great, Iris! What's your secret? They were comments that fueled her forward, made her think she was doing a great thing.

Iris thought about the phone calls she got from her own grandmother after she'd been admitted to the clinic, who wished her well in a roundabout way and asked how she was as if she'd been down with the flu. She thought about what a cancer patient's room looked like on television: full of flowers, balloons, bedside vigils. Cancer patients were unfortunate, brave, fighters.

She thought about the certain possibility of death. A death nobody could blame you for.

Megan said, My alternative? She looked at Iris. A fucking cold.

Sally, the oldest girl in the group, the kind who wore black eyeliner and lace-up boots, laughed a loud, open-your-mouth-with-your-head-back laugh. Iris held her breath.

Megan had never said fuck before.

Dr. Leincroft chose to ignore it.

Kissing Was the Horrible Image of Herself

Six months after her discharge from Ellentower, Iris got a boyfriend. Alex was a senior and they met in advanced placement biology. When he first asked her out, she told Megan, He's so not my type. But then his dirty blond hair and dimples grew on her, despite the fact that he was shorter than she was, despite the fact that he had seen every episode of *Star Trek: The Next Generation* with his parents, despite the fact that he had never been to a football game, ever, and she lived to kick her legs beneath the powder blue and white miniskirt with the Lakeridge logo in front of a whole stadium of fans.

Iris's mom walked around smiling and laughing again, as if Alex in her daughter's life was proof that her daughter was healed, would help her feel confidence in her body as it was.

Her father said, I think I've cleaned his parents' teeth. Good people, seems like.

Megan said, I can't believe you let that dork stick his tongue in your mouth. She said, Don't even think about adding his weight in with ours. We'd be freaking huge.

At night, after the football games, or the movies, or a rented video in her parents' living room, Iris and Alex drove around Lake Oswego. They stopped in the lower parking lot at George Rogers park, getting out to stand on the bridge if it wasn't raining, staying in the car if it was. Kissing was nothing like Iris imagined it to be. Kissing was a chore that kept Alex from getting bored with her, a wet, strange ritual that tasted like Alex's dinner if they hadn't had chewing gum in the car. Kissing was a quick hand on the stone-cold skin just above her waist, just under her shirt. Kissing was the gentle pressure of Alex's hand along her thigh, the growing boldness of his fingers as they inched toward her bra, its hook in the front.

Kissing was the horrible image of herself, someday, naked in front of somebody else, her flesh everywhere. It was driving home in silence, trying not to cry herself to sleep at night. Kissing was a thing she could do on an empty stomach only, the thought of a heavy, warm stomach between her and him as loathsome a thing as she could imagine.

On the phone, even to Megan, even to herself, she said: God, Meg, I could kiss him all night.

In unison, one hundred and ninety-four pounds together, Megan and Iris breathed.

What Megan Wore

When Megan was discharged from Ellentower, she wore the same outfit as the day she was admitted: an apple green sweater from Banana Republic with a matching striped scarf, khaki pants with a front seam from Express, and black ankle boots with a square toe. Megan liked to think of herself as fashion conscious. She'd had small side bangs cut a month earlier, because she'd noticed Britney Spears had them, and wore only a translucent pink lip gloss and Pink Barely There blush on what the cosmetic companies called the apples of her cheeks.

When Megan was discharged from Ellentower, they had her come back every weekday for twelve weeks, nine to five. Her least favorite tutor at the center was a robust woman in her midforties who kept telling her that when she went back to school, she'd be ahead of the game. She said it with an explanation point, like this: Great work, Megan—when you get back to school you won't just be caught up, you'll be ahead of the game!

When Megan was discharged, she showed up at Ellentower as an outpatient every morning, ready to strip down to nothing and step on the scales, ready to have every ounce of her food weighed, every movement of her body tracked to check for calories consumed and calories burned. She thought about calories in very concrete terms, as if they were little bugs that could enter and leave her body at will, little creatures that could eat her from the inside out.

The Dentist Suggests Fuddruckers

Iris lost five pounds her first week after being discharged from Ellentower. On a Saturday morning, when she would have liked to be standing next to her mother's friends as they read *Vanity Fair* on the treadmills and StairMasters at Club Sport, she left the house with her father to run some errands. They went to Safeway to pick up eggs and ricotta cheese for her mother. They went to Fred Meyer so her dad could buy new batteries for his digital camera. While there, Iris had to stand with him in line while he bought KY Jelly to use in his dental office, and she stared hard at the ChapSticks and batteries next to the register out of embarrass' ment, in case anyone her age saw her father buying sex products.

When they climbed back into the front seats of her dad's Acura, he suggested hamburgers at Fuddruckers for lunch.

Iris said, I'm not really hungry.

Her dad was silent. And then he turned to her, and she could see that he was crying, and he started telling her everything she already knew about anorexia, everything she was risking, and he said, So you're coming to Fuddruckers with me to eat hamburgers, or I'm taking you back to Ellentower.

Iris felt her very bones, which she had previously thought were made of fragile glass, light up from the inside out. It was a re' action that surprised her—surprised her that, after thriving for so long on comments about how skinny she was and people freaking out about her weight, it was this all-lit-up feeling of having some' one actually love her, having someone actually say, I'm scared as hell and I'm not letting this get worse, that she felt might save her.

But for the Blind Date . . .

But for the blind date with Alex's best friend, Iris would never have seen Megan puking. Alex's best friend was tall and dark haired, the type of boy Megan always had crushes on. Iris and Megan met the two boys at the cinema in Wilsonville, because stadium seat' ing was important to Alex. The four of them stood in line while the boys ordered two large tubs of popcorn, Jujubes, Junior Mints, and four regular sodas. Neither Megan nor Iris dared ask for diet.

In the dark, in the movie theater, in the middle of an action scene, Megan thought: What if he gets upset that I haven't eaten a thing? What if I eat some popcorn and it ends up stuck between my teeth, and it turns out I don't have floss in my purse? She'd seen a television show once where a girl and her date reach for the popcorn at the same time and end up holding hands for the rest of the movie. So she ate a whole box of Jujubes instead, and most of the Junior Mints. Megan excused herself and stood to use the restroom. When Iris realized Megan had gone, she followed after her, hoping to find out how Megan felt about Alex's friend.

Iris was waiting for Megan when she came out of the bathroom stall, having heard everything.

Iris did not have to say: When did you start purging?

Iris did not have to say: I am pulling in most of our one hundred and ninety-nine pounds.

Iris did not have to say: Do we even weigh one hundred and ninety-nine pounds?

Concerns You Might Have about Group Therapy

The handouts both families received the day their daughters were admitted to the Ellentower Clinic for Disordered Eating addressed common concerns about group therapy. In bold type, at the top of the page, it said: At Ellentower, never will we mix children with pure restricting anorexia and those with binge/purge anorexia in the same group to avoid children getting "ideas" or picking up new behaviors.

The handout said: These two groups of children meet at different times and both are always under the supervision of the adult group therapist who directs the conversation during the session.

The handout said: Group therapy is an invaluable part of your child's treatment and recovery, and we will ensure it is a safe, effective environment.

What the handout did not say: When your child and her best friend recover at different rates, they will hate each other and love each other, fiercely, at any given moment.

Iris and Megan Imagine Alternatives

When Iris and Megan had gone three weeks without seeing each other because of school, and because of Alex, and because of having been placed in different groups at Ellentower, Iris called Megan on the phone to invite her over. It was a Friday afternoon, early May, and they sat on Iris's bed with their legs crossed, taking a quiz out of *Seventeen* magazine. Megan said, let's do something wild.

Iris said, Like what?

Something out of character, Megan said.

Out of character?

Yes, out of character. Megan did an impression of Dr. Leincroft: Let's imagine some alternatives, she said, her voice deep and mocking.

Iris said, Okay. I'll be a gorgeous blond with legs up to here. She put her hand up to her neck.

Megan said, I'll be the kind of girl who can dress as slutty as she damn well pleases and doesn't care who looks at her.

Good plan, Iris said. They grabbed their purses and left in Megan's car without saying anything to Iris's mom. Megan drove to the Washington Square mall and parked near the food court. They shopped at Nordstrom, The Gap, and Banana Republic, because Megan liked the tall, flat-chested models from Banana Republic and the Gap and Iris liked the perfectly together middle-aged models in the Nordstrom catalogs, who reminded her of the women on the treadmills at Club Sport. But they finally both settled on outfits from Abercrombie and Fitch, mostly because they knew the store had shocking nude catalogs, and in this alternative, they were that kind of girls.

Megan bought a layered tank top and low-waisted miniskirt. She didn't even have to lift her arms for her stomach to show. Trying it on, she looked into the dressing room mirror and stared at the flesh-colored stripe around her middle, the stripe of skin against fabric, and thought: In this alternative, I think I look fantastic. In this alternative, I am not going to demand a baggy tee shirt over the top, a jacket to tie around my waist.

Iris looked at Megan in the mirror and noticed how much thinner she'd become in the last few weeks, the dark circles under her eyes. She thought, I am on the other side of it now. And then, almost instantly, she hated Megan for it—she saw herself only growing bigger and bigger, her flesh ever expanding, while Megan continued to get thinner. Megan left to buy her outfit, and Iris tried on the items she'd grabbed—camouflage capri pants, white halter top, white strappy sandals with a three-inch heel.

In this alternative, she thought, my best friend is heavier than I am, and she envies my cinched waist, my perfect ankles, the way I can disappear under size zero tanks. Iris found herself unable to turn around and look at herself in the mirror once she'd put her outfit on. Even in this alternative, she knew, she couldn't hold the fantasy: she would notice how much wider her hips were than Megan's, how much pudgier her stomach.

They wore the clothes out of the store and climbed back into Megan's car. Iris said, Let's go shopping at the new Lakeview Village. Let's eat dinner in these clothes at one of those new restaurants that just opened. But Megan's car stalled out just as they coasted into the parking garage off A street, and when she turned the key in the ignition, it wouldn't start up again. Iris said, I'll call my Dad, but Megan wouldn't let her. She said, Let's not ruin the night. She thought, but did not say, After all, how often are we normal?

Iris suggested walking home, but they both thought about wearing their new outfits all the way home, about the looks from the passengers in passing cars, and decided without saying anything that walking was out.

Megan said, Let's call a cab.

Iris said, They have cabs in Lake Oswego?

They have cabs everywhere, Megan said.

So cab it was. After they ate at Manzana, after they window-shopped to their heart's content, they called the first cab company they found in the phone book and told the dispatcher they would meet him in front of *Sur La Table*, the gourmet kitchen store on the corner of State and A streets.

By then the dusk had settled around them and every so often they were hit by a pocket of cold air, a reminder that it was not yet summer. Iris thought about the clothes she had sitting in Megan's car, the clothes she'd left the house wearing earlier that night, but she didn't dare be the first to recommend they change. Every few seconds, the headlights from the cars turning at the intersection illuminated the corner where they stood, the light stopping briefly as it dragged by, as if a spotlight, as if pausing to take in the two awkward girls on the corner in clothes they wouldn't ordinarily be caught dead in. Megan wrapped her right arm around the stripe of flesh at her midriff, and Iris crossed her arms and put her hands on the thickest part of her bare arms. Goose bumps rose from their skin. Flanking them on each side was a terra-cotta pot, bursting with blue grasses and red flowers.

And then it was dark, completely, except for the light from the store behind them and the traffic lights alternating between red, yellow, and green. And then it was cold, too, not just occasionally chilly. And then it had been almost half an hour since either of them had spoken.

Together, almost in unison, Iris and Megan thought, We haven't added our weight in weeks. I wonder how much we weigh.

They turned toward the sound of footsteps from the sidewalk to the left of them. A police officer approached them, his face hard as stone, hand on the equipment hanging from his hip, wanting to know what they were doing on the corner of State and A. The breeze blew the grasses in the pot in front of the officer, but nothing else seemed to move.

In unison, having no idea what they weighed together, Iris breathed deep and Megan stared straight ahead, her face set and hard as the terra-cotta pots on either side of them.

Robert Horncroft, Naked

Reporting party says a resident of the 600
block of 1st Street goes out into the fenced
yard naked.

—*Lake Oswego Review* police blotter

Police received a report of a naked man running on a path by the Willamette River at
George Rogers Park. The man was described
as white and in his 40's.

—*Lake Oswego Review* police blotter

OKAY, SO YEAH: you might have seen me naked.

Used to be, in the days before my wife went missing and I
was a real important guy, next in line to make partner at my firm,
I loved the feel of fabric against my skin. Truly, when you're on
top of the world, does anything beat the starched press of cotton
menswear stripes against your flesh, the even, heavy weight of a
suit coat spread across your shoulders and down each arm? I have
been accused of many things, but hear this now: it is not true, this

charge that I hate clothing. Ask any of my former clients. Show up in court, I'd tell them, dressed for the part. A few I dressed in my own suits. When Milt Freeman was acquitted, I was so happy I let him keep my cuff links.

Carrie used to like wearing my button-up shirts, before she up and vanished. On hot nights she'd roll the cuffs to her elbows and wear them buttoned only from her navel down. What man doesn't like seeing his woman in his shirts, smelling her in the fabric after she pulls her shoulders through the top and steps out of them? That's something else: the way smell clings to fabrics. Nothing holds a smell so well as clothing. The beads of scent hold fast to the threads and refuse to leave for anything. Before we were married, when Carrie and I were still in college, she got the notion to make herself a skirt out of men's ties. We scoured garage sales and made trips to Value Village, and when she had enough she pulled the filling from each one and sewed them together, edge to edge, and wore it with a pair of thick winter tights. But I hated for her to wear it: I hated that she smelled like so many other men, that they all had private access to that glorious part of her that I would bury myself in, piece by piece, every day if I could.

There were a few things that disappeared along with her, mostly her nicer clothing. And three of my button-up shirts, the three she wore the most. To the police this was proof she left of her own will, but I know better. Carrie had no reason to leave. Oh, sure, we had our moments, but she's my girl. Leaving just isn't in her nature. I wanted the works: I'd seen it done before, when a beautiful young blond thing goes missing and they pull out the search teams, the community volunteers, pepper the state with fliers and cadaver dogs, search the state parks and the landfills. But I had to put up fliers with Carrie's picture on them all by myself, and it was so hard for me to do that I only got a few up around my neighborhood and then some on the other side of Lake Oswego, fliers with a picture of Carrie from our honeymoon on the front and my name and phone number in big pleading letters along the bottom. I got a few calls. Mostly from old clients and sympathetic friends, wanting to know how I was holding up, wondering if I'd heard from her. That sort of thing. Nothing you could organize a search party with.

Can I say how it felt to come home and find her gone with my best shirts? I didn't even realize there was a problem until it neared ten o'clock and Carrie still wasn't home. I called her cell phone and got a series of empty rings, not even a prompt for voice mail. That's for the best. The sound of her voice in a recorded message might have done me in. I walked through our entire house, which wasn't hard. We were still in the nine-hundred-square-foot, vintage First Addition home we bought my first year out of law school, the home we'd sworn to keep only until we had children and could build on the lake. Anyway, I walked through every room of the house and I took stock of what was gone and what wasn't, and I knew something terrible had happened. I woke the next morning to the sound of my radio alarm, and in the nanosecond it took me to focus my eyes I thought it was any old morning, and that it was time to shower and dress for work, but then I reached my arm to my left and remembered: no Carrie.

I could not bring myself to dress. It's really that simple.

Every item of clothing I had felt like a burden. What could I put on my skin that wouldn't hide the need I felt to find her? I felt like I was four again, when it was all I could do to keep my clothes on, the itch of the fabric and the tags on the nape of my neck a horrific wrong. Every so often I run into an old friend of my parents, someone who remembers me running down the aisle at church in the middle of the service, shedding pieces of my clothing as effortlessly as a bird loses feathers, pew after pew as I passed. It came back to me the morning after Carrie disappeared. The need to be alive in my skin. To feel the air against my body, to feel the goose bumps rise up along my arms and legs, the free movement of my sex as I walked. I didn't dress all day. I walked to my front gate, leaned over the fence to pull some weeds as tall as the four-year-old me I was just now remembering, and got my mail.

I pulled myself together. I went to work the next week again, the same suits on my body I'd worn for years. But they felt different, in a way that might be impossible to describe. You know that feeling you get, when the weather changes slightly and you stand back and look at the sky as if you've never seen it before, as if you have no idea what it might do next. I felt that way about my clothed self, as if my body didn't belong there, as if anything could happen.

And every now and then I let him out, that little Robert, that four-year-old, and we go for a run by the river at night, or I creep down to an empty dock at the lake and I look at the water under the Northwest sky, and I let the air take my skin, ride over my chest and my bare ass like ribbons, and it's like I can be new again if I try hard enough. And then sometimes I'm standing there and I remember how much Carrie wanted to live on the water, and I think about us, about how I was, and being naked is not enough for that. I only ever laid a hand on her once, in all our years, and how can I say sorry for that? I would step out of my own skin and let the whole world see the gray of my bones, the red strings of my muscles, if it would bring her back. Really, I would.

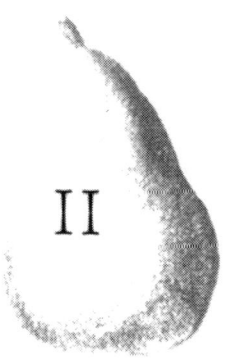

II

Mountain Park

Crabwise

Vandals broke lights at an apartment complex
Jan 12th on the first block of Monroe Parkway.

—*Lake Oswego Review* police blotter

THERE WERE DAYS when the four of them sat in smoky theaters downtown to watch obscure bands play until after midnight. They laugh about those days now, how they sat for hours nodding along to bands with names like Belly Under and Crabwise, and how sometimes Marguerite and Brenda even let their husbands smoke, and sometimes even smoked themselves. Now Marguerite's husband works for a company with a box in the Rose Garden, and if they listen to live music it's from the comfort of Suite 75, fully catered, all-you-can-drink pop in the fridge and red wine if you want to buy it. Last year they saw Bette Midler and Paul Simon, the year before that Billy Joel and Melissa Etheridge.

Tonight it's Sarah McLachlan. Before the show starts, Marguerite says she's hungry for real concert food, hot dogs and nachos instead of crudités and cranberry turkey wraps, so Nathan and Jim leave the suite to find the concession stands below. While they're gone, Marguerite and Brenda pour root beer into glasses with ice, and Marguerite sits down in a leather bucket chair with her feet propped up on the table.

Brenda laughs. "Make yourself at home."

"Are you kidding?" Marguerite leans her head back, spreads her arms out and lets them drop over the sides of the chair. "This is like heaven. Four hours ahead of loud grown-up music, nobody pulling at my shirt to nurse or begging for a sip of my drink." She lets out a long exhale. Brenda smiles and walks to her seat overlooking the stage, and Marguerite feels a thin film of guilt sweep over her. She's usually better at this. She's had five years, after all: five years since her oldest was born and Brenda started infertility treatments. Marguerite can usually read her friend's moods enough to know when it's okay to mention her children, to ask about Brenda's treatments, or to keep her mouth shut altogether. But even in their best moments, when the world melts away a bit and they are the old friends they've always been, laughing in sync and finishing each other's sentences, flirting with each other's husband, even then there is something that hangs over them, a subtle constant in the background: Marguerite got kids and Brenda didn't.

Nathan and Jim come back into the suite just as the lights dim and the crowd below them erupts in screams and applause. They've brought pizza and popcorn, not what she asked for, but Marguerite knows if she complains Nathan will roll his eyes and make a crack to Jim about high-maintenance women. And then Sarah is taking the stage and they all sit down, and it's too loud to talk, and Marguerite has missed her chance to apologize to Brenda. Next to her, Nathan shoves a piece of greasy pepperoni pizza into his mouth and then dabs at his fingers with a napkin. From the corner of her eye, she sees Brenda on the other side of her, sitting with Jim's hand on the inside of her thigh and her fingers rubbing his lower arm. She's always surprised by this, by the way Jim and Brenda have a romantic ease about them. The ease of a couple without children.

They leave in the middle of the first encore to beat the crowds, just after Sarah and her lead guitarist sit on the edge of the stage together and sing a cover of "Blackbird." From the backseat of Jim and Brenda's Land Rover, Marguerite laughs at Jim's criticism of the set, the song choice, how commercialized good music has become. They all listen to Jim tell his famous story about the time he saw Elton John from the third row, about the way Elton paused during "Crocodile Rock" and pointed right at him, looking in his eyes, and smiled, as if he knew a true music connoisseur when he saw one.

There is silence after Jim speaks. Marguerite watches the city pass as they head back toward Lake Oswego. The freeway follows the river, the bridges spanning its width like carefully chosen accessories. And then Jim's voice again: "So it turns out I have like the world's most useless sperm." Marguerite can see Brenda's face in the rearview mirror: expressionless, her skin smooth and sad. She pictures Jim's sperm as oddly shaped little blobs, swimming in aimless circles, and curses herself for having to stifle a smile.

*　*　*

Three weeks later, Brenda and Jim ask for Nathan's sperm. The night begins normally, with Marguerite cutting Brenda's hair in her kitchen while Nathan and Jim work the grill outside. Owen barrels through from the family room wearing nothing but a diaper and lands in a pile of Brenda's hair. Marguerite picks him up by one arm, the scissors still balanced in her right hand, and tells him to slow down. He toddles out onto the deck with the hair still stuck to the backs of his chubby thighs.

Brenda says, "Remember when Brittany used to run around here wearing nothing but diapers?" Marguerite combs Brenda's wet bangs down against her forehead, forcing her to close her eyes while she continues, "I can't believe she's ready to start school."

Marguerite nods. "It is strange, isn't it?" She takes the texturing shears into her right hand and snips away at the ends of Brenda's hair where it hits just below her chin. She says, "Hell, remember when I could cut your hair in an actual salon and not on a kitchen stool?"

Brenda laughs. "This is much better," she says. "Less pressure to tip." Marguerite laughs as Brittany sulks into the kitchen with a clear Polly Pocket case in her hand and her lower lip thrust out theatrically.

Brenda leans forward and says, "What's wrong, Sweets?" It strikes Marguerite as strange that Brenda would call Brittany "Sweets," the name that Marguerite has used to address her daughter since she was born. Brittany shrugs and says, "Owen ate Polly Pocket's *purse.*"

Marguerite feels a touch of panic and says, "He *ate* it? Are you sure?" She looks outside where Owen is bouncing on his dad's knee, giggling each time Nathan pretends to almost drop him. She says, "Britt, hon, how big was it?"

"*Mom!* He ate her purse! He needs a time out."

Marguerite says, "I'm sure he didn't mean to do it, Sweets. Go see if Daddy needs help." Brittany slams her right foot to the floor and then walks sluggishly through the sliding glass door.

After Brenda's hair has been swept off the kitchen tile, after they have consumed roughly four shish-kabobs apiece, after Owen and Brittany have been reluctantly put to bed, the four friends sit on the back deck sipping drinks with their shoes off. Brenda clears her throat and starts, "We want to ask you something." Marguerite looks away while Brenda describes the exact problem with Jim's sperm, that their only option is donor sperm, and that they'd rather have a donor they know than one they don't. "Less surprises, gene pool-wise," Jim says jokingly.

"Of course, take your time," Brenda says.

"Yeah, yeah," Jim chimes in, "Think about it, that's all."

Marguerite stands to clear the table when Nathan grabs her hand. "Why would we need to think about it? If we can help you have your baby, we're all for it," he says. "Consider it yours."

Brenda looks at Marguerite. "Are you sure?"

Marguerite smiles, almost convinced. "It's just sperm," she says, "I mean, of course." She collects their bottles, holding three to a hand, and tries to believe she isn't bothered by the idea, the way she has tried to believe all night that she shouldn't be worried about a hard pink plastic purse the size of a nickel lodged somewhere in her toddler's digestive tract.

* ⋎ *

Marguerite seems to be the only one bothered by the prospect of the sperm swap, so she keeps her mouth shut. They all speak about it in easy terms, as if it's the most normal thing in the world, as if Nathan is lending them gasoline, or extra peanut butter. Each time her husband emerges from their bedroom with a brown paper sack and hands it off to Jim, the clock running, something new occurs to her. She thinks about all the potential babies in that bag, siblings to Owen and Brittany, guilty that she feels such a claim over the most microscopic parts of her husband's body.

She thinks about what will happen next in an uninspired examining room at Brenda's doctor's office, about how the microscopic parts of Nathan's body will be inside her best friend. She looks at Jim carefully, watching for a meaningful glance, an understanding in his face that he, too, is bothered by the connection that is forming between their spouses. But he, like Brenda, seems all hope and glow at the prospect of a child.

Marguerite and Jim kissed once, late, after seeing Crabwise play in a bar downtown. Brenda was in the bathroom and Nathan had gone to get the car, and they'd all had too much to drink, and Jim leaned toward her and they both went in for it, the kiss. Kissing Jim was like landing on a planet she'd only seen through a telescope, barely; like touching the red rocky surface with her feet and then being quickly pulled back to her ship. It had happened fast, and never went away. In the years since, every so often, they look at each other across a table or from the other side of a grill and remember.

It's a connection she relishes, late at night, alone, and hates in the light of day, one she dreads seeing form between Brenda and her own husband, if only from the sterile mingling of their bodies.

    ✳ ✳ ✳

Brenda is one of those cute pregnant women, someone who actually seems to glow, like a supernal, motherly being. Her belly is low and perfectly round, and Brittany likes to touch it with both hands and say, "When your baby moves out it's gonna be round, round, round," and laugh hysterically.

For Brenda's baby shower, Marguerite decorates her house in pink crepe paper and ties packets of pink Jordan almonds with a lacy ribbon, for favors. Brittany helps her use a cookie cutter to make sugar cookies shaped like little feet, and Marguerite paints each little toenail with pink powdered-sugar icing. When the guests arrive, they sit around Marguerite's living room in a semicircle, Brenda perched in the leather armchair like royalty, collecting gifts at her feet. Mitzi, who lives down the street and is the president of the PTA at Brittany's school, insists each woman give Brenda a piece of advice before she opens her gift.

Mitzi goes first: Sleep when the baby sleeps.

Jen, Brenda's cousin, tells her to keep a regular date night with her husband.

One of Brenda's coworkers tells her to always put the baby down awake.

Then it's Marguerite's turn. Brenda holds Marguerite's gift in her lap, wrapped in white paper with little pink footprints stamped along the seams. Playing the perfect hostess, Marguerite is refilling the punch bowl when she feels all eyes on her. Her mind races through everything said to her when Brittany was born, everything she's learned in the five years since she became a mother. She thinks about saying: Frozen bagels are great for teething, or Use lanolin cream on your nipples after each nursing session, or even, You will never be the same person again, ever, so don't even try. But each piece of advice that runs through her head brings with it a picture of Brenda with a baby tucked under her chin, gently, a baby with Nathan's green eyes and Nathan's turned-in pinkie toe.

She takes the easy way out. "Choose the epidural, and choose it early on," she says, and the room erupts in laughter.

Later, after the guests have all left and Nathan and Jim have come home with the kids, Marguerite lets Brittany and Owen talk her into watching a Barney videotape before bed. Jim sits on the couch between them with his arm around Owen while they watch, and it isn't long before his eyes close and he's sleeping silently between her children. She glances at them occasionally while she picks up the paper plates from the table and the torn wrapping paper, cramming them into a white kitchen trash bag. From the television, Barney and his young cohorts sing a song about cooperation.

She grabs two trays of food from the table and carries them into the kitchen, where she finds Brenda and Nathan leaning over the counter, their shoulders touching. When they look up,

Marguerite can see the object of their rapt attention: a string of black-and-white ultrasound pictures, fuzzy photographs where Brenda's fetus looks like a blob floating in a mess of black ink.

It isn't the pictures that startle Marguerite, exactly. It's the look on their faces: guilty, as if caught. Nathan tugs at the already loosened knot of the necktie he has yet to take off. Marguerite imagines their expressions would be the same if she'd walked in on Nathan unbuttoning Brenda's blouse or kissing her neck from behind. They had been sharing a moment, wondering about the unborn child that is a mixture of their genes, and she had interrupted it.

At midnight, long after Brenda and Jim had left with garbage bags full of baby paraphernalia to make the short walk down the hill to their house, Marguerite lies in bed next to Nathan. She looks at him without completely turning her head, out of the side of her eye, and she can see his profile as he lies looking at the ceiling, unblinking. She finds herself playing the part of the insecure wife, wondering what he's thinking. By the time he turns toward her she is willing, anxious, even, to feel the weight of his body.

Their lovemaking is nothing out of the ordinary, nothing outside of their regular routine. After so many years, Marguerite can predict which part of her body he'll gravitate toward and for how long, and she responds as predictably. She slides underneath him and, thinking of Brenda's distended stomach, remembers what it was like to try to keep up their sex life during her pregnancies, the shifts and changes they had to make to accommodate her bulging abdomen. However her body was changing on a daily basis, the stasis of Nathan's body was always a comfort to her. His has always been the explored, known landscape, the kind of place you want to return to and sleep against under nothing but sky.

* * *

Fiona is the other woman, from the first minute she is born. It's something Marguerite wasn't expecting. But every time she sees Brenda press Fiona to her breast, every time Jim straps her against his chest in the baby carrier, every time Nathan offers her one of his enormous fingers to clasp with her pink, newborn hand, something behind her rib cage twists and burns. She has a hard time watching Brittany lean over Fiona's baby seat, cooing, without feeling a sense of envy. It occurs to her that she is the only one who isn't connected to Fiona by blood or parenting.

When Marguerite decides to hold a "welcome to kindergarten" dinner for Brittany, Brenda and Jim bring Fiona in her removable car seat and a three-layer chocolate cheesecake. Marguerite can't help noticing, as Brenda bends underneath the banner with Brittany's name on it (the one Marguerite strung across the dining room) and carefully unstraps Fiona from her harness, that Brenda's every movement seems easier, happier. It would be fair to say she shines. When Brittany was born, Marguerite remembers six months of crying jags and sudden panic, six months of wondering what she'd done to separate herself so drastically from her former life, six months of the tingling that rose on the back of her neck every time Brittany cried or woke too early. But Brenda is a poster mother, the kind of mother who makes everything seem easy. The kind of mother, Marguerite thinks, other women rip to shreds on *Oprah* for making the rest of them look like bad parents.

Brenda sits in a dining room chair and lifts her shirt like an old pro, barely moving while Fiona latches on to nurse. Owen runs through the dining room and stops at Brenda's chair to rub Fiona's hairless head. "Fona nurney?" he says.

Marguerite laughs at the way he still uses the term for nursing he adopted when he was fourteen months old. "Yep, that's right, Owen. Fiona is getting some nurney." She turns to Brenda. "Is she still nursing well? Are you sore?"

Brenda shakes her head. "Never really got sore. Lucky, I guess." From the living room, Jim and Nathan break into laughter over something they see on the television, and Owen runs from the room to follow the sound. Brenda goes on, "We've decided we got such an easy one as payment for all those years."

Marguerite can't help herself. "Is that how it works?"

"It's a joke, Marg."

Brittany walks in before Marguerite has to explain herself and twirls in a pink corduroy jumper. "Brenda, I'm starting kindergarten tomorrow!" She tucks two little blond strands of hair behind her ears and touches Fiona's tiny hand.

Brenda says, "So I've heard. Excited?" Brittany nods her head and leans over awkwardly to rub her cheek on Fiona's hand.

Marguerite finishes with the silverware and pats Brittany on the backside. "Leave that baby alone—she's eating." When Brittany leaves the room, Marguerite says to Brenda, "Sorry. It's just all this, I guess," she gestures with her hand around the dining room. "One minute you're desperate for a cure for colic, and the next she can read the word 'cat' and is starting school."

Brenda unlatches Fiona and pulls her shirt down. Marguerite holds the back of a dining room chair and watches the milk dribble from the side of Fiona's mouth, a look of exquisite bliss on her doll-like face. As Brenda raises Fiona to her shoulder and pats her back, she says, "So it really is as fast as they say, huh?"

It isn't a question meant to be answered. But Marguerite would say: Sometimes yes, and sometimes no.

Sometime toward the end of dinner, as they are all finishing their homemade macaroni and cheese (Brittany's request) and Marguerite is taking a washcloth to the wall of the dining room where Owen threw his, Fiona starts to cry. Brenda looks slightly alarmed and stands with the baby in her arms, bouncing around the room to try to soothe her. For the next hour, they take turns. Jim walks outside with her and tries to distract her by pointing out flowers and trees. Nathan suggests strapping her into her car seat and placing it on top of the washing machine, which only makes her scream harder. Marguerite holds her firmly around her middle and slowly bends and unbends Fiona's knees, remembering how night after night she had to do the same when Brittany screamed as an infant.

Marguerite tucks Brittany and Owen into bed and then the four adults take Fiona out on the back deck, where they can see over the top of the house below theirs into Lake Oswego, where the lights have started to come on and the town looks tranquil, but alive. It's what Marguerite loves about living so high on Mountain Park, that she can feel like she is straddling both worlds: Portland, her old urban life, which she can see from the front porch, between the houses across the street, and upper-class suburban calm from the back. But Fiona is altogether unaffected. Brenda's eyes start to tear over, and Marguerite feels a sense of justice. Try every night for months, she thinks, and then tell me about motherhood. What she says out loud: "I'm sure it's just gas, or something you ate that she's reacting to." And when Brenda's expression doesn't change, she adds, "She's fine, honey. This is what babies *do*."

Still, within half an hour, Jim and Brenda are in the car, on the way to the emergency room at Meridian Park Hospital. Marguerite clears the plates from the dining room and rolls her eyes conspicuously when Nathan walks through.

He says, "That's not fair."

"Excuse me?"

"Do you remember what that was like? The first baby? You were scared shitless for months."

Marguerite pauses, drops three plates loudly into the sink, then says, "You were completely indifferent to her before."

"Fiona?"

"No, Nathan. Brenda."

"Before what?"

Marguerite turns her back and scrubs the plates, listening to Nathan's deep sigh, a signal that he's willing to let it go. "The emergency room?" she says. "Babies cry. A couple of gas drops, she'll be good as new."

But Nathan isn't so sure. "I'd be worried, too. Fiona's different," he says, "she just doesn't cry. I don't know. It's different."

An hour later, when Nathan takes his Seiko from on top of the dresser and fastens it around his wrist, the way he does when he's going out, Marguerite gives him a questioning look. He tells her he just wants to check in on them, lend support, see how things are going at the hospital.

Marguerite lies on their bed and clicks on the television, flipping through channels without registering what she's seeing. As Nathan leaves the room, she says after him, "She isn't your child."

Nathan pauses in the doorway. She notices his thick neck and his small shoulders, framed against the darkness in the hallway. He says, "That's the funny part, isn't it?"

When the phone rings, she doesn't know how long she's been asleep, and her mind is so hazy she isn't sure if it's Jim or Nathan on the other end. He says, "Fiona's fine. Constipation. Go back to sleep, honey." And she does.

* * *

Winter break, Nathan takes a week off to be home while Brittany is out of school. They call it their "vacation at home." They all sleep late, even Owen, and during the day they go to the science museum or to the mall to see Santa, or they sit at home and have a fire in the fireplace. Nights, they let the kids stay up late and watch movies while they all pile onto the king-size in their bedroom. On Christmas, they stay home for the first time, instead of driving to Washington to open presents with Nathan's family or with hers, and they let the kids talk to their grandparents on the phone and they decide not to clean up the wads of wrapping paper until after they've eaten lunch and watched the kids play for a while.

Still in her bathrobe, her feet on the coffee table where Owen is rolling a plastic fire engine back and forth, Marguerite says, "Does it feel like we're in a Norman Rockwell painting?"

Nathan laughs. "This week, yes. Most weeks, though, Picasso."

Marguerite thinks of people with blue bodies whose limbs are all mixed up, musical instruments you have to squint to find, and she nods her head. Nathan breaks up a fight between Brittany and Owen, who have begun throwing balled-up tissue paper at each other. Then he sits back down on the couch next to Marguerite and asks, "Are we going to walk down and see Jim and Brenda today?"

Marguerite doesn't say anything. It's been over two months since they have all been together, something that Marguerite chalks up to Brenda being busy with a newborn and Marguerite spending so much time volunteering at the elementary school. Isn't that, after all, what happens? Don't people just simply grow apart? But somewhere hidden, in an almost tangible place inside her head that Marguerite thinks she could touch if she were brave enough, she knows it's something else. The dynamics have shifted. She wonders if they crossed some strange boundary of friendship that shouldn't have been crossed, some line beyond which healthy friends know not to go. And it isn't just her: Nathan, even, finds it hard being around Fiona after Jim and Brenda started letting her cry herself to sleep at night. It breaks his heart, he says, that a baby who is, let's face it, sort of his, feels a nightly torment he would never allow his own children.

"We'll call and say Merry Christmas," Marguerite says. But soon they forget all about it, and the day slips away, and they eat turkey and banana cream pie, and Brittany and Owen fall asleep in the living room like spent toys run out of batteries. Nathan pulls Marguerite into the room to look at them, sleeping with the tops of their head almost touching, and whispers, "Norman Rockwell." He stares at them a long time before he motions for her to help carry them off to their beds, long enough that Marguerite can't help but wonder if he senses someone missing.

And then they are two weeks into the New Year, and Nathan is back to working every day, and Brittany is sitting with her nose pressed to the window because it has started to snow. They'd watched the forecast all week, hoping for a few flakes. It's been three years since they've had real snow in Lake Oswego, long enough that Brittany doesn't quite remember what it's like. She points out the biggest flakes she sees and Owen runs onto the back deck without his shoes on, laughing hysterically and looking to the sky, his eyes squinted. When Marguerite runs after him with his boots and coat, he's got flakes stuck to his lashes. She bundles Brittany up, too, and then watches through the glass while they both patiently hold their palms open to collect what comes from the sky.

Through the sliding glass door, Brittany yells, "What if there's so much snow that Daddy can't drive home from work?" Marguerite shakes her head and yells back, "Daddy will be fine. It isn't supposed to snow that much, Sweets."

But by noon, there are three inches in the driveway, and the entire deck and lawn are spread with an overlay of white powder. Soon, the kids tire of playing outside and they return to their regular routine, until Nathan comes home early and shakes a dusting of snow off his black patent leather shoes when he walks in from the garage. Brittany yells, "Daddy!" and he says, "I wanted to make it home before it got any worse."

After dinner, they dress in their warmest clothes and go for a walk. Nathan ties a line of thick twine to the lid of the garbage can and pulls Brittany along behind him, and when they crest a hill so steep that it frightens her, he sits on the lid himself and slides to the bottom. Brittany and Owen find this hysterically funny. At the top of Monroe Parkway, Nathan loads Brittany and Owen onto the lid while Marguerite cringes nervously, and Brittany holds Owen soundly around his middle while the snow descends in swirls around them. Just as Nathan pulls on the twine, they hear someone call out to them.

The snow is coming down in thick, wet flakes, so much of it that in the light of dusk they don't see anything but two figures coming toward them. But Marguerite recognizes Brenda's voice, recognizes her heavy gait as she and Jim approach. Soon they are close enough to see, and they exchange hellos in the dim light. Brenda's got Fiona strapped to her chest in a baby carrier, a pink knit hat pulled low over the baby's forehead to protect her from the cold.

"Brenda! Look at me and Owen! Daddy's *pulling* us!" Brenda laughs at Brittany's obvious glee, says, "Yeah, I can see that."

Brittany turns to Nathan. "Can Fiona get on, too?"

"Britt, Fiona is kind of little still," Nathan says, "but that's nice of you to ask."

Jim looks at the mild slope of Monroe and says, "She'll be fine. Pop her out, Bren."

Brenda doesn't move. She squints her eyes at Jim and then brushes wet flakes from the top of Fiona's hat. She says, "I don't think so."

Marguerite holds her finger out to Fiona, who takes it in her hand and pulls it to her mouth and sucks hard. Marguerite says, "I'm with Brenda on this one. I don't even like Owen on that thing."

Jim dismisses their concern with a wave of his hand, and Brenda stands still as he lifts Fiona from her carrier. Fiona kicks her legs with excitement and lets out a burst of pure laughter, grabbing at the snow. She sits straight up inside Brittany's legs next to Owen, who wraps his arms around her. Jim looks at the fence just to the right of them, the end of a small deck off an apartment complex with white lights strung loosely across the top and around a tiny shrub at its base. He finds the end of the lights and wraps it around all three kids, who laugh as they watch the twinkles swirl around them.

"There," he says, "it's a little After Christmas ship."

Brittany says, "Uncle Jim, I can't move my arms!" Fiona grabs at the strand and shoves it greedily into her mouth between giggles. Marguerite sees for the first time her husband's left dimple on Fiona's face, the almond shape of his eyes.

Nathan says, "We're not going to get very far like that." But as Jim goes to unwrap them, the lights become snagged and tangled, and when Jim yanks harder, something in them gives and the whole strand—along the fence, around the tiny shrub, up the side of the tall complex—goes dark. "Whoops," Jim says. "We better get out of here." He winks at Brittany.

Something in the look he gives Brittany, in the mischievous tone of his voice, reminds Marguerite of the old days, the days when the four of them felt like they could do anything, could drink as late as they wanted, back before the kids when the world was theirs alone. Marguerite can't remember the last time she and Jim looked at each other as if to remember that night they heard Crabwise play. She can't remember the last time she noticed Jim and

Brenda with their arms around each other, practicing their romantic ease with public display, and felt a pang of envy because her own husband was so publicly stand-off-ish. She wonders if that's what she was most angry about after Fiona was born—not that she was part Nathan, but that her birth signaled the end of something.

When Jim and Nathan get the kids free of the lights, they pull the makeshift sled down the street, so quickly that Brenda and Marguerite are left behind trying to keep up. Marguerite misses the ease with which she and Brenda once walked, the time when she wouldn't have thought to care if Nathan's fuzzy ski cap, pulled low over her brows, made her look ridiculous. For the first time, shoulder to shoulder with a woman she once knew as intimately as herself, Marguerite knows they won't get it back.

Ahead of them, Jim and Nathan are playing like schoolchildren, taking turns tugging the garbage lid through the snowy streets. Marguerite sees them framed in the darkness, the two men who once seemed to hold opposite parts of herself. That night in the bar, Crabwise had played the same cover they saw Sarah McLachlan play—"Blackbird," all acoustic, their normally grunge voices softer, purer. And they'd been a little bit drunk. And Jim had kissed her. And they'd crossed a line, then, too. And she'd hummed the song all the way home, thinking, *take these broken wings.*

They see the little sled come to a stop a few yards ahead of them. Marguerite hears Owen crying: his scared cry, not his hurt cry. She knows by the intensity and pitch of his screams. Through the snow, someone comes toward her with Owen in his arms—Jim or Nathan, she can't yet tell which—and she rushes forward to comfort her child.

Moon over Water

A resident of the Parkridge I apartments on
Greenridge Drive says he can't go on to his
back porch for fear of being attacked by a
vicious cat.

—*Lake Oswego Review* police blotter

I WON'T DENY that a full moon is wondrous beyond description, especially in western Oregon, where in the right areas the dense green fir trees reach so high you'd swear the tips of their branches could kiss the moon in all her full-bodied, blue-tinted glory. It is a sight to behold. Some nights I drive to work with my sun roof open, trying to see it from every possible vantage. The community college is at the highest point in town: the top of Mountain Park, on old Mt. Sylvania. From the mathematics building, where I teach, you can look down at the lights of the surrounding cities as if they are fallen stars. But even up there, the moon doesn't look any bigger, and I don't feel any closer to its mystery. Night after night, regardless of which part of town I find myself in, the moon looks exactly the same: a smug glistening orb, round and smooth as polished stone. It's always just over the next bend, just past those trees, just on the other side of the water tower.

Tonight, my students seem uninterested, melancholy. The number on my roster is dwindling: sixteen where there were thirty-two at the beginning of the term. This is not a surprising thing. Ninety-three consecutive nights of full moons has wreaked havoc on more than just Introduction to Statistics. As a statistician, I hold to my belief that human beings are a superstitious people. We are no more affected by the changes in the moon's phase than we are by random chance. Study after study has proven no increase in suicides, death rates, tragic accidents, psychotic episodes, even, during a full or new moon. But when the moon stops cycling altogether? Problems arise. We've seen that now, firsthand.

I call on Tran Lee to start off our problem review. The other students look around, shake their heads.

Tran is gone, they say. Tran went east last week.

And like that, we've lost another one to the moon. People are leaving the Portland area in droves, heading east to where you crest the highest point of the Cascades and there, suddenly, is an entirely different moon, one that still varies its distance from the earth, its shape, its brightness and color. New moons, crescent moons, waning gibbous moons.

Statistically speaking, our moon has to change sooner or later. I'm waiting it out.

* * *

My wife, Mary Grace, is already home from her shift at the hospital when I pull into the garage after class, tired and ready for sleep. I find her in the family room, hovering over our daughter's guinea pig cage. She puts a finger to her lips and motions me forward.

"Quiet," she says. "It's happening."

"Again?" I ask, and look into the cage. I can see Bubbles, the brown and white female, straining while she lies on her side. Two little baby guinea pigs have already been born, and clearly she's working on a third. It's one of the strange things that's begun happening since our moon froze, completely full, in the night sky. All of our pets have been in a constant state of fertility. In our neighborhood alone, there have been five litters of puppies and seven litters of kittens born in the last three months. Our dog Mugslee, a tiny fawn pug, has started to round about the middle and move with a maternal, deliberate caution, despite being spayed three years ago. Male animals have begun pacing the streets. Even the tamest of male pets have developed an aggressive streak, un-settled by the preternatural state of the night sky. One of my cal-culus students told me that he can't even walk onto his back porch without being blindsided by a vicious calico who lurks in his bushes.

Even we are not immune. I'll confess to an increased sense of amorousness. I think about my wife as if we were newlyweds again, imagining us in new and exciting positions while I sit at the front of the classroom, waiting for my students to finish a quiz. But Mary Grace is no fool. She doesn't want to end up like Bubbles and Mugslee, so she keeps her distance, sometimes even sleeping on the floor of our daughter's bedroom.

And there are other peculiarities: the plants have been grow-ing at an inordinate rate, especially here in Lake Oswego, where we pride ourselves on our green landscapes. Hostas that ordinarily are only a foot and a half tall have grown in excess of five feet. In my own yard, I have a line of purple and yellow foxgloves along the walk that have already reached seven feet. Their blossoms, which ordinarily look like little upside-down thimbles, large enough to fit my thumb, are now the size of small drinking cups. I swear, if I tried hard enough, I could fit my fist into some of them. Most of our lawns need to be mowed every other day. Ferns need to be trimmed in order that their fronds stay below fence lines. If the moon doesn't start cycling soon, we will be in for a bountiful fall harvest: watermelons big enough to bathe in, corncobs the size of my whole arm, pumpkins kingly enough to rival the one that carried Cinderella to her fateful ball.

Next door, Mr. Huffaker, an eccentric old man who lives in his garden from March to October every year, at first found this intoxicating. I'd wave to him as I walked to my mailbox, and he'd be laughing to himself. He'd call out to me, "Hot damn, Tony, have you seen this tulip?" and he'd stand next to a blossom that matched him in height and was roughly the same size as his head. Soon, he was buying every growing thing he could get his hands on at the Lake Grove Garden Center and planting them on his lot, until there wasn't a spot of bare earth to be seen. It was something straight from a fairy tale: vines running here and there, foliage twisting around foliage, arcing above the fence, the mailbox, the house, even. And then Mr. Huffaker disappeared altogether. I realized I hadn't seen him in days when I ran into his daughter and son-in-law, hacking their way to the front door through the jungle he'd created. To this day, they haven't found him. I like to think of old Mr. Huffaker living off the strawberries and green beans inside one of his bamboo-stake teepees, laughing at the rest of us for our inability to adapt to this new world.

Bubbles has begun making the kind of loud squeal you'd associate with dying, not with birth. Mugslee, meticulous in her stride, comes over to take a look inside the cage. On her little pushed-in face is a look of terror. Mary Grace lets out a laugh.

There are five baby guinea pigs, in all.

Outside, we know without looking, is the moon: a stationary, regal voyeur. Unrelenting. I see it after I go to bed, in my sleep, when I should be dreaming of guinea pig babies and calculus problems: the moon, reflecting sunlight the way Navratilova returns a serve.

*   *   *

I drive up to campus for my morning class, sometimes having to veer the car toward the center line where inattentive homeowners have failed to trim their plants back to the curb. I have heard that some of the more rural parts of the county have had roads completely overtaken by vegetation. As I leave my neighborhood, I notice on the end of the street a pink bleeding heart, its soft fernlike branches outstretched in four- and five-foot arcs. From the underside of each branch, the blossoms dangle in the perfect shape of hearts, large enough, I think, to replace the one beating inside my chest. It's these small surprises that have probably kept me here the past three months, despite all the strangeness.

On the radio, a nationally syndicated talk show has dedicated its hour-long program to dissecting the "Portland Moon Problem." An astronomer with a deep, measured voice sounds baffled by the entire thing. "It's completely illogical," he says. "There's no evidence the sun has changed, no interruption in the rotation of the earth. We have yet to find a real scientific explanation." Another scientist chimes in with his theory: "In my lab," he says, "we are looking at disturbances in light and atmosphere. This will clearly turn out·to be a trick of the eye, a sort of mass optical illusion." The astrologer, a new-age woman who sounds like the type to wear crystals and carry tarot cards, disagrees, asserting that the people themselves have created the problem out of a need to get in touch with their places in the universe, their spiritual selves.

The spokesperson for a leading Christian organization dovetails onto the end of her speech: "It is linked to spirituality, yes, but not the kind you speak of. This is a wake-up call, a sign of the last times."

A sign of the last times, my ass, I think as I pull into the faculty parking lot. Why, for example, would the rest of the world not be experiencing the same thing? If God wanted to begin ending the world, would he not start with regions that are notorious for sin? Las Vegas, say, or Hollywood? A student from my calculus class stops me as I approach my office.

He scratches his head and looks over my shoulder instead of directly into my eyes. "I was hoping to get an incomplete for this term," he says.

"Any particular reason, Kevin?"

"Going east," he says. As he says it, I notice that he looks drastically different than he did only a few weeks ago. He has gained a considerable amount of weight, and the extra flesh on his cheeks and chin makes him look several years older. I nod my head, sign his little blue slip, and watch him as he walks away. I put a hand to my waist. I've noticed only in the last week that I've had to put my belt buckle through different holes to loosen it up. Mary Grace says I'm probably just bloated, that she's experiencing the same thing. The full moon's pull on the tides, gravity being affected, that sort of thing.

It's a strange sense of doom I'm feeling, and I try to shrug it off. I open the door to the mathematics building and head straight for my office, all the while knowing that if I turn around and look hard enough in the blue sky behind me, I will be able to see the faint suggestion of a perfectly spherical moon; an apparition watching us, always.

　　·　·　·

My sister Jeannie, who calls almost daily from Denver out of a distorted need to know about the strange effects we've noticed about town, phones me at my office and says, "I read in our newspaper that four pilots are missing and some of the old-growth firs are growing so tall they make creaking noises."

"That's true," I tell her, wondering where she hears such nonsense. "Just this morning, in fact, as I left for work, some of the trees in my yard began to creak, and then I realized they were actually speaking to me."

Jeannie says, "You are an ass."

"You make us sound like some sort of freak circus show over here."

"Aren't you? Anyway, I really called to tell you that you can come stay with me for a while, if you need to." I balk a bit at this, insisting to her that I am unaffected by the mass hysteria and don't need to be rescued. But I thank her for her offer, and before I hang up the phone, there's something I need to know.

"What does it look like there?" I ask.

"Last night? Waning gibbous," she says, describing the phase when the full moon has abated, the lopsided circle that shrinks nightly until it's a crescent, then almost disappears altogether. I miss that moon. But there's one moon in particular I miss the most: the waxing crescent, when the moon appears as no more than a flicker of eyelash in the night sky.

* * *

If you look closely for too long at the face of the moon, it starts to play tricks on you. You see things on its surface that you know are utterly ridiculous, completely impossible. The visible face of the moon has gradations of light and dark that some people say resemble distinctly human features, while others think it looks like a rabbit or a dog. Mary Grace swears, when she looks just so, she can see a swiftly running horse, its mane flying backward with speed. My daughter Emily, in all her six-year-old innocence, sees a slimy gray monster with huge hands. Sometimes she asks us: "Remember when the moon used to get skinny, like a potato chip with a bite out of it?"

When I look at the right time of the night, the face of the moon looks like the profile of a majestic old woman. I can see her pointed chin, her salient brow, a little button nose. I can see plumes of feathers framing her face, as if hanging from the brim of her hat.

All of the stores in the Portland Metro area have sold out of telescopes. They have become the hottest gift item. But Mary Grace, who works in admitting at Meridian Park Hospital's emergency room, won't let Emily or me go near one. She says she sees patients every day with strange burns around the edges of their faces, as if the moon drew them in through the instrument, determined to leave its mark. Even after the burn heals, she says they are left with a pale, otherworldly glow to their faces. She likes to point people out in public places who've spent too much time staring at the moon through a telescopic lens: "That man over there, in the corner booth," she'll say. "And look at the burn marks around her eyes—there, behind the cash register."

Still, I can't help but think I'd like to get my hands on a telescope, just once. I want to know what that woman is doing up there, the whole moon to herself. I want to know if she's smiling or grimacing. I want to know what color those feathers are.

*   *   *

I pick Emily up from school on my way home from work. She's standing out front with a row of first-grade children, their teacher at the end. I have to drive past a line of bright yellow buses before she spots me and we exchange waves. It's as she approaches the car that I finally have to admit to myself she's changing, too. Her walk is slower, her ankles thick and swollen. She's wearing one of my wife's old tee shirts because her own clothes must not fit. In fact, Emily is on her way to being one of those children they exhibit on talk shows to condemn our nation's propensity to turn out obese kids. People in the audience would scream at me and chastise my decision to let her eat hot dogs on a regular basis. I shift in my seat and lean over to unlock the passenger-side door for her. The movement is distinctly uncomfortable, because the extra rolls of flesh at my sides and under my arms make swift movements harder to perform.

We are growing at alarming speeds.

Mary Grace comes home from the hospital with Chinese take-out from the Safeway deli. She waddles in—I'll admit it's the first phrase that comes to mind. My wife, always a petite little thing, is now becoming my charming little fat wife. She looks at us, alarmed by what she sees, and then takes a deep breath and grabs some plates from the cupboard. After dinner, Emily plays in her room while Mary Grace and I search for answers.

"I still think it must be tidal," she says. "If the moon can cause the whole ocean to move, why not the water in our bodies, too?"

But I ask her to consider something else. I want her to consider that our bodies might be cycling themselves, taking up the slack where the moon left off. This sends Mary Grace into fits of hysterical laughter.

"Are you listening to yourself?" she says.

"This is no crazier than anything else going on around here," I defend myself.

"So we're growing, filling out, like the moon?"

"Yes," I tell her. "Technically, we're waxing gibbous." Her laughter dies down, but I can tell she is giving it some thought.

There are questions to consider, possibilities we don't want to address out loud, if I am right.

By the end of the night, Mary Grace and Emily have packed their things and are ready to leave for Jeannie's place in Denver. But I can't bring myself to go just yet. I want to ride this out. I tuck them safely into their safety belts—all their extra flesh—and stow their suitcases along with Bubbles and her babies. Mugslee stands at my calves as I wave them off, sending them in the direction of the luminous moon, completely at its mercy.

* * *

My evening statistics class is down to eight students, most of them bordering on obese. Statistically speaking, I have calculated, by the time the term is over, none of these students will remain to receive a grade. This makes it hard for me to put any real energy into my lectures, or spend much time grading problem sets. I let them go early, and walk to the faculty parking lot. To get there, I have to use my pocketknife to hack away at the ground cover that is nearly twelve inches high and has taken over the sidewalk since I arrived three hours earlier. The campus has taken on the look of a South American rain forest, the buildings scarcely visible for all the lush green that grows faster and faster each minute that passes. I snap off the branches from an overhead maple that are sitting on top of my car, then climb in without even attempting to fasten my seatbelt. I tried this morning and failed: the thing no longer fits.

I've been lonely without my girls. Without them at home, there's little to keep me sitting around the house, and I've taken to mindless driving. Tonight, I head north on Interstate 5 toward Portland with no particular destination in mind. The freeway is practically barren. I reach for my pocket and pull out my cell phone, then dial Jeannie's number. Mary Grace answers. She sounds genuinely happy to hear my voice, and I ask how she is.

"Almost back to my pre-moon weight," she says, then giggles. "Comes off fast." She wants to know when I'm coming, worried, I can tell, that I'll wait too long and she'll lose me.

"Soon," is all I can seem to muster. She puts Emily on the phone.

My voice gets jovial: "How are you, ladybug?"

"Great! Aunt Jeannie has three cats. And I'm skinny again."

"Sounds fun, honey."

There's a pregnant pause, and then: "Dad?"

"Yes, bug?"

"The moon here is a small sliver, like a bitten-off fingernail."

By the time I hang up, I am in the heart of downtown Portland. On Sixth and Salmon, a group of rioters has gathered, and they're screaming with their fists in the air. Large, every one of them. I wonder what the cause is this week, knowing this is nothing unusual for Portland. Then I notice that some of them are dressed in costumes that look like silver moon crescents, and they are holding signs that say, "Don't blame the moon" and "The moon is a victim, too."

And I think: We are a silly, silly people.

I make my way through the crowd and head back to Lake Oswego, the moon behind me. I can see it in my rearview mirror, a bright, omniscient eye, propelling me forward. I want to see this moon over water. I want to see what it will look like hovering over Oswego Lake, suspended above the murky water by some sort of heavenly puppetry. When I reach the bridge on South Shore Road, I'll pull to the shoulder and admire the way the moonlight blankets the water with a muted, otherworldly, light. I'll look for that old woman's reflection in the light that stretches from dock to dock.

What will it be like, I think, if I ride this cycle out to its destined conclusion?

What will it be like, this death by moon?

I think of Mr. Huffaker, buried alive somewhere in his fairy-tale garden, the house now long since gone. And I wonder if his body is doing the same as mine. I am waxing gibbous. And soon —days, maybe, from now—I will be full bodied, at my maximum, in all my cycled glory, before I wane in size, become gibbous again, then a thin, silver crescent, then nothing.

Stealing Yakima

A woman reports her estranged husband
came to her house while she was gone and
took their dog.

—*Lake Oswego Review* police blotter

HERE IS BRIAN PALMER, dressed and ready for work, and here is his two-year-old daughter in his bed, still asleep, her stomach barely moving with each breath and one hand resting above her head. He watches her for a moment and then backs out of the room, closes the door slowly, and steps lightly down the stairs. His mother is already in the kitchen, scrubbing his dinner dishes from the night before. She's already opened the living room and kitchen blinds, though it's still dark outside. Even so, Brian can see water clinging to the other side of the glass and knows it will be wet again.

"When did you get here?" Brian asks, reaching for his mug.

"Ten minutes ago, fifteen maybe. She sleeping?" Brian thinks about Charlotte, her two-year-old breaths on his pillow, and nods his head. His mother grabs the pot of coffee and fills his cup where he holds it out to her. He thinks he should tell her not to do his dishes, that he can take care of things like that himself, but he knows it won't make a difference. His mother puts the last dish in the dishwasher, slings the gray dishtowel over her shoulder, then pulls a novel from her purse and sits at the kitchen table. From the baby monitor on the counter, they hear the swish of wet tires on pavement every time a car drives past the house.

"I have an appointment today," she says. "I'll need to take Charlotte, but it won't be too long." Brian nods his head in agreement and finishes his coffee quickly. If he leaves before Charlotte wakes, it will be easier to get out the door. He walks to the breakfast nook out of instinct, ready to fill the dog's bowl, but stops himself when he sees the empty dog bed and remembers that Yakima, along with his wife, is gone.

Brian steps into the dark rain and starts his car. He knows his mother will hear him—as he releases the emergency brake, as he backs from the driveway and into the morning rush out of Mountain Park, as he accelerates in the direction of the high school —all in a circle of sound: the baby monitor in his bedroom upstairs, tuned to its highest sensitivity, will inhale the sounds and spit them out again somewhere in his kitchen, where his mother sits turning the pages of her book and slowly sipping her coffee.

*   *   *

When his wife left with Yakima three weeks ago, it would have been full light already at this time of the morning. And she had left in the morning, before he and Charlotte were awake, in that first light. At the time, he felt mostly confusion that she had left and anger that she had taken their dog, which they'd found abandoned five years ago along a stretch of highway just south of the Washington city that bears its name. As the weeks have worn on, through the beginning of spring and twenty-one nights and mornings, he's become more angry for Charlotte's sake than for his own. What kind of mother takes the dog but leaves the child? What kind of mother leaves at all?

His first visit to her new place went badly. She'd taken an apartment in Pipers Run, a unit of duplexes at the forested end of Child's Road, in the part of Lake Oswego that isn't Lake Oswego at all, but county land. She was in an upstairs unit, the top end of a duplex, and he climbed a full flight of steps covered with moss and almost slipped twice. The place was dark, curtains drawn, but when he knocked Yakima appeared in the window next to the door, jumping up between the curtain and the glass, whining and barking at the sight of Brian on the front mat. Through the dirty glass, Brian admired the swish of his dog's long dreadlocked fur. His wife opened the door and he looked at her as if seeing her for the first time. She appeared as if days had passed since she had combed her hair or dressed. Empty milk cartons and newspapers crowded the kitchen table, and the apartment smelled of mold and old animal stains. Brian glanced around the place and then back at his wife. He told her they could find her a better place to stay if she still needed some time.

"You aren't paying for this," she said, "my father is." She looked up at him and lit a cigarette. "Do you want to go through it again, Brian?"

"Through what?"

"Through the part where I tell you it isn't about you. The part where I make it clear I don't know what the hell I'm doing."

Brian was silent for a long while, then said, simply, "And Charlotte?"

She laughed, then met his gaze. "Look at me," she said. "One step away from those women on the news with long hair and no makeup, the kind who wake up one day and drown their kids in the bathtub." She stopped laughing, said, "I don't want to do that."

His wife sat on the floor then, and Yakima sat with her, his head in her lap, while she stroked the dog's charcoal dreadlocks with her free hand. And looking at her like that, Brian thought: How unoriginal. He could have painted his wife from an article he'd read in a waiting-room magazine with the title "When Mothers Can't Cope: Postpartum Depression and the Twenty-First-Century Mom." He had a hard time believing his wife's problem because it was so textbook, something she could have copied from a million other women in their color-coordinated kitchens. But then he thought about his wife: that uncontainable energy that so quickly disappeared after Charlotte was born, the way she used to squint her eyes when she smiled. Her situation *was* different. She had grown to feel as trapped by him as by their child.

Yakima looked up at Brian and wagged his tail. Brian called Yakima to him and let the dog lick his face, jump up onto his knees. He'd come with the intention of convincing his wife to come home, or at the very least of taking the dog with him, but at the last minute, the courage he'd come with had gone. He guessed nothing he said could get her to come home. And he guessed he liked the thought of Yakima snuggled close to his wife, keeping an eye on her.

*　*　*

Brian is at the high school within five minutes, and by the time he parks his car, the rain has slowed considerably. The parking lot is mostly empty, but he knows as the sky lights up and another hour passes, it will fill with other cars, most of them student cars nicer than the one he drives. He accepts this as part of the reality of being a teacher in the Lake Oswego School District, where he and his colleagues joke that many of their students have allowances greater than their own salaries.

He walks into the high school slowly, passing Kay at the front office desk and offering a hello. He unlocks his classroom and then the English department cupboard, pulling stacks of books from the top shelf. He'll start a new unit with his sophomores today, so he counts out sixty-four copies of *My Ántonia* into stacks on his desk. Half of the copies are the edition he fell in love with when he wrote his honors thesis on Willa Cather in college: the edition whose cover shows a picture of a single plow illuminated by the sunset. His notes on Cather he pulls from a manila folder and sits to read through them, when he hears a tentative voice from the door: "Mr. Palmer?"

A student from his freshman class is standing in the doorway, half in and half out, her whole body a question. Every sentence she speaks is a question, too. "I'm here for my makeup test? I was sick last week?" He should know her name; it's April already, after all, but the only names that come to mind are the characters from the notes in front of him.

"Of course, right," Brian says and waves her in with his hand. He runs his fingers through his file box until he finds the exam and gives it to her with a forced smile. She chooses a desk in the front, directly on the other side of his, and places the exam and a phone on top of it. The phone looks like the kind that can take pictures and do other spectacular things. "I'll use a pen?" She pulls a blue ballpoint from her backpack. Brian nods his assent and the two settle in to their separate tasks. He is surprised to find he likes how it feels to have someone else in the room with him. He likes how much smaller the space seems. He looks at the empty coffee mug on the corner of his desk and wonders if Charlotte is awake. The girl sighs and scratches something out with her pen. Her phone beeps and she looks at it, briefly, and smiles at something she sees, probably some text message from a boyfriend just now arriving at school.

Claire. Her name is Claire.

*   *   *

Brian and his wife found the dog along the highway after visiting relatives in Yakima. His wife had fallen asleep as soon as they had started out, and he had thought she was still napping when she started screaming, "Brian, stop! Stop! Pull over!" He eased the car to the shoulder of the highway and they found the dog in the bushes fifty yards behind them. Brian held out his fist the way he'd been taught and lowered it gently under the dog's nose so the dog could smell him. The dog tilted his head to the right and then licked Brian's knuckles.

They tried to get the dog to stand, but he limped severely on his hind leg. His fur was rough and matted near his face, but the long dreadlocks still hung off some parts of his body, and Brian could tell that if the dog was cleaned, those dreads would be the color of the highway asphalt underneath them. Brian's wife buried her face in the dog's fur and said, "What this poor dog must have been through," and Brian said, "Must be one of those Hungarian sheepdogs. Never seen one in person."

By the time they carried the dog to their old Civic and settled him into the backseat, his name was Yakima. A veterinarian in Portland put Yakima's hind leg in a cast and shaved some of the most matted spots of his fur, making him look as if he'd survived a major battle. They made a bed for Yakima in the living room out of their best blankets, and Brian held his paws while his wife worked to get the antibiotic capsules into the dog's mouth and down his throat. Brian went to bed early, worn out from the day, but his wife fell asleep next to Yakima, her arm slung across his back. That's where Brian found them in the morning, and he made coffee as the dog sat up in its makeshift bed and wagged his tail and they all laughed and felt like a family. Brian put his hand on his wife's thigh and loved her so much he felt like a newlywed again. He kissed her cheek. "I guess he's pretty lucky we found him," he said, and scratched Yakima behind his left ear.

* * *

Third period, Brian is reading the prologue to *My Ántonia* out loud to his sophomores when Kay comes into the classroom. "Sorry, Mr. Palmer," she says, and beckons him to follow her into the hall. Brian looks at his students. He puts one of the girls from the front row in charge of reading where he left off and closes his classroom door behind him.

"Sorry, Brian," Kay apologizes again, "but your mom keeps calling. She says your little girl won't stop crying. Wonders if she feels well." Brian sighs and nods his head. He uses the phone in the office to call his house and tells his mom that Charlotte is probably cutting molars, that she can give her some Tylenol drops from the medicine cabinet. He hurries back to his classroom and finds them finishing the passage just in time for him to launch into a discussion about first-person narration and the role of the narrator in Cather's novel.

By the time the bell rings, his stomach is churning and he's ready for lunch. But Kay stops him on the way to the teacher's lounge to tell him his mother is on the phone again. He makes his way to the front office and puts the receiver to his ear. His mother's voice: "She's fine, Brian. She's asleep. Wanted to let you know." There's a pause on the line, and then his mother says that his wife had called. "She claims she needs some cash and that she's leaving town for a while. I don't know, honey, I think you should call her."

Three of his students pass him and call out his name. "Yo, Palmer!" And he answers back with a smile. He thanks his mom and hangs up the phone. He heads back to his classroom, forgetting his hunger, and loses himself to his notes about *My Ántonia*, to wheat fields in the Midwest and the book he admired for its realism before he had any problems of his own. And he's suddenly struck with the idea that he wants to get away, that he wants to take Charlotte and leave for the weekend, to do something away from the house with the mortgage he can't afford, and away from his helpful mother, from the empty dog bed in the breakfast nook.

* * *

Two weeks after Charlotte was born, Brian's wife refused to get out of bed, refused to nurse the baby. Her breasts became hot boulders that would occasionally leak circles of milk onto her clothes. She stared at the ceiling with Yakima's head on her stomach while Brian danced around the kitchen with a fussy Charlotte, learning how to test the heat of formula on his wrist and squeeze the air bubbles from a bottle. On the third day of this, his wife, who hadn't smoked for years, asked for a pack of cigarettes and let the tears stream down her face after she'd lit the first one. Yakima clambered up the bedsheets and licked the first round of tears off her left cheek before she pushed him away.

And two weeks later she got out of bed, showered, and cuddled Charlotte in the crook of her elbow. She said, "I think I can do this now," and Brian didn't question. His wife was back and he tried not to think of losing her again until she and Yakima disappeared in the early morning. Sometimes, late at night, in the dark, he wonders if they were ever in the house at all.

* * *

By skipping out on his last-period prep, Brian is able to get to his house in Mountain Park by two o'clock. Charlotte has just awakened, and there is still sleep crusted in the corners of her eyes.

Brian sends his mom home and then grabs the small suitcase from the closet—the only piece of luggage his wife left behind. He packs three changes of clothes for each of them and whatever toiletries he sees nearby, and they are in the car by three, heading for the coast. Brian feels almost giddy, being so spontaneous. He doesn't know where they'll sleep, doesn't know, even, which coastal town they're headed to.

While they're being spontaneous, why not? Brian decides to stop off at his wife's place to see if he can persuade her to come along. He makes faces into the rearview mirror and Charlotte giggles, sticking her tongue out in return. When they get to Pipers Run, he leaves Charlotte in the car where he can see her and runs up the steps to the apartment. Yakima is in the window before Brian reaches the top step, so instead of knocking Brian tries the door and finds it unlocked. Yakima jumps up on him, panting, goes for Brian's face with his huge tongue. When he looks up, Brian doesn't see his wife in the living room or kitchen, so he figures she must be behind the closed bedroom door. He contemplates going in there after her, but changes his mind at the last minute. Instead, he takes Yakima by the collar and leads him outside. They are only halfway to the car when he can see Charlotte pumping her legs up and down with excitement, bouncing her arms off her knees at the sight of the dog.

"Yaki! Yaki!" She's screaming when he opens the car door and guides Yakima inside. The dog puts his front paws on either side of Charlotte's car seat and licks her face while she squeals in delight.

Brian looks at them in the backseat and says, "Well, guys, should we go?" Yakima looks at him and Charlotte laughs.

What he didn't expect was that Yakima would miss his wife. They are barely to the freeway before the dog has propped his paws against the window, whining. The whole ride to the beach, he paces the rear of the car, as if he's nervous, as if they've left something precious behind. Yakima finally settles in to sleep by the time they head north on Highway 101, but soon Charlotte begins to fidget and cry, wanting out of her car seat. Brian is prepared for this one: he has fruit snacks and cheese puffs in Ziploc bags on the empty passenger seat beside him, and he tosses them to her, one after the other, to keep her contentedly chewing for the rest of the drive.

He pulls from the highway at his first sighting of the ocean. It's not even five o'clock, and he's pretty confident he'll be able to find them a motel somewhere along the highway, in any one of the impending coastal towns. But there's been a sudden clearing of the sky, and he wants to take advantage of it. He wants to feel the sting of blowing sand on his face and touch the chilled ocean water. He wants to watch his dog run again, Yakima's long fur swaying rhythmically as he strides.

As soon as she realizes Brian has pulled off the highway and is parking the car, Charlotte starts yelling, "Out, Daddy, out!" and tugging at the straps of her car seat. She yawns as he frees her from her buckles and transfers her into the metal frame backpack from the trunk of the car. When he straps her on his back, she tugs at the top of his hair with her tiny fingers. He pulls one of Yakima's leashes from the glove compartment and then the three of them are off, following an old trail in the direction of the water.

Charlotte falls asleep in minutes, lulled by the bounce in Brian's walk and the sound of the waves as they approach them. Brian hikes down a large dune and finds himself on a long, empty beach. In the distance, at the tip of a peninsula, Brian can make out the old lighthouse, and not too far before that is Haystack Rock, an immense boulder rising above the water like a newly hatched island. Beside him, Yakima whimpers again and looks behind them in the direction of the car. The dog plops down in the sand and rolls onto his back, as if to feel the sand in his fur. Brian laughs and lets go of the leash. He slowly eases his arms out of the backpack, and then pulls Charlotte from it with gentle tugs, careful not wake her. He lies down next to Yakima with his baby girl on his chest, the sand damp beneath him, and closes his eyes.

When he opens them again, he knows he's been asleep for some time, and he instinctively grabs for Charlotte on his chest, but she's gone. There's a split second when he thinks he must have dreamed the drive, and Yakima, and the ocean air, but he can hear the waves, and knows that as soon as he sits up he'll see miles and miles of sand. He jumps to his feet, panicked, and realizes Yakima is gone, too, and he knows the dog must be with Charlotte. He yells the dog's name and scans the horizon, frozen to his spot on the sand because he doesn't know which direction he should head.

But then he sees off in the distance, in the same line of vision as Haystack Rock, a pair of dark figures that must be Yakima and Charlotte. The sun behind them has started to set, so they look like silhouettes. He sees Charlotte put her arms around Yakima's neck and fall backward on the sand, then stand up again and jump, as if they're playing some game. He walks toward them slowly, feeling a strange calm. As he gets closer, their figures grow larger and larger in his vision, and soon the sky behind them is filled with the orange light of sunset, and his girl and his dog look like the illuminated plow on the cover of *My Ántonia.*

Charlotte is laughing as he approaches, and seeing her face up close makes Brian's heart pound for the first time as he becomes aware of how close he could have been to losing her. The sky feels as though it's getting ready to rain again, and his entire back side is wet from his nap on the damp sand. Yakima barks playfully and starts to run parallel to the surf, his one bad leg a split second behind the even rhythm of the others. And Brian Palmer thinks, A kid needs a dog. And he knows, scooping Charlotte up in his arms and chasing after Yakima, that they might never get his wife back, but the dog, the dog they'll keep.

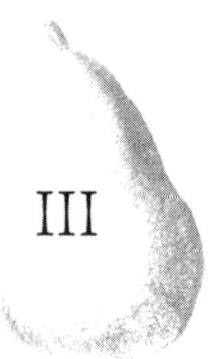

III

Lake Grove

Vital Organs

Food was thrown at the garage door of a home.

—*Lake Oswego Review* police blotter

A Nugget the Size of a Golf Ball

HOLLY'S LEFT KIDNEY began disappearing on a Tuesday. She's pretty sure of the date because, in retrospect, she remembers feeling a strong sense of loss over something she couldn't exactly pinpoint, a sad yearning as if from her very bones. And then a week later, after a nasty bout of the stomach flu prompted her doctor to check for gallstones, she was lying on a hard metal table counting ceiling tiles. When the sonographer found something "of interest," she was sent to x-ray, an even colder room with an even bigger metal table, and then to the radiologist's office, where a handsome young man with auburn hair dramatically removed his glasses and told her the facts. The good news: her gallbladder was in tip-top shape. The bad news: they were unable to locate the top fourth of her left kidney.

He stood and clipped four x-rays to the light box beside his desk. The first two were of her right kidney. He kindly pointed out the telltale bean shape, the soft, healthy look to it. The next two were of her left kidney: sure enough, a nugget the size of a golf ball looked as if it had been bitten off by a voraciously hungry creature. In its place was nothing: empty space where a kidney chunk once had been. The handsome doctor offered that perhaps it had always been this way, or maybe something was quite wrong. Either way, she was to check in with a nephrologist in the morning.

It was a puzzlement. That night, she left her daughter Jane in front of the television and made up enough tuna casserole for several nights, placing half of it in the freezer. If something happened to her, at least there would be food. When her husband came home, the three of them sat in the dining room, tuna, noodles, and peas spilling onto their plates, and ate in silence. She watched Jane use her fingers to pick out the peas and place them delicately in her three-year-old mouth, wishing she'd named the child something more exotic, like Xiola or Violet. A name like that would linger, long after a person's various parts started inexplicably vanishing.

Holly leaned back from the table, rubbing her left side where her shrinking kidney sat.

"You okay?" Kevin was smiling.

"Just tired." It was then she remembered the previous Tuesday, the feeling of longing that accompanied her when she woke for the day, the sadness so much like grief that made it hard to stir Jane's playdough, to make the beds, to answer the telephone. She'd missed that small, spongy piece of herself without even knowing it had gone.

The Best Part about a Kidney . . .

The nephrologist at St. Vincent's Hospital was a robust man in his midforties named Dr. Whitney, who smiled after almost every sentence. Holly decided this was probably because in his field there was so much bad news to dispense, so much worry to alleviate, that he had to develop a permanently cheerful disposition. While Jane played quietly in the corner, he drew countless vials of her blood, stared at her x-rays for a full ten minutes, left the room and then came back, and then left the room and came back again.

"I don't know what to think," he said, then smiled. "I mean, I'm not sure I've seen anything like it."

Holly said, "Oh." Jane stood on her tiptoes until she was able to reach a small plastic kidney sitting on the counter next to the sink.

Dr. Whitney continued, "Do you feel pain in your lower left quadrant? Inability to urinate?"

"Nothing." Jane dropped the kidney on the hard white floor and the sound reverberated through the small office.

"Jane," Holly said sternly. "Be careful with the doctor's things."

Dr. Whitney smiled. "No harm done," he said cheerfully. He knelt down in front of Jane and cradled the kidney in his palms. "Can you say kidney?" he asked. When she didn't answer, he pulled at the kidney's side until it opened on hinges, revealing a perfect cross section of veins and arteries. Jane ran her finger along one of the veins while the doctor said, "The best part about a kidney, young lady," he smiled at Holly, then looked back at Jane, "is that you have two of them."

Holly was sent to the bottom floor of the hospital for another immediate, more comprehensive x-ray. The staff in radiology was kind enough to entertain Jane while technicians injected Holly's veins with blue dye and took pictures of her body from every angle, some with a pillow under her, some not, some with her rolled up on her side, some not. Then the tech left the room. When he returned, he removed a sterile-looking black telephone receiver from its cradle on the wall and handed it to Holly.

"Hello?" she said, wondering who could possibly be calling her here.

"Mrs. Martino?" the voice on the other end belonged to Dr. Whitney.

"Yes."

"It seems the rest of your kidney has vanished." Holly said nothing, puzzled. The doctor continued, "We'll wait for your labs to come back and have you in on Monday for more tests, unless something happens over the weekend."

Holly said, "Where did it go?"

Dr. Whitney sighed. "Honestly, we have no idea." She could hear him smiling.

Lipstick on the Mirror, a Bloody Back, Etc.

On the way home, Holly and Jane stopped at the Lake Grove Garden Center, where Holly knew paperwhite bulbs would be ten for ten dollars. She'd made it a habit to plant paperwhites just after Thanksgiving every year, and she intended to do the same this year, defunct kidney or no. Jane helped her count the bulbs (skipping the four and the seven, as usual) and place them in a brown lunch sack. After paying the man at the register, Holly loaded a bag of white planting pebbles and a few small decorative pots into the back of the station wagon, buckled Jane tightly into her car seat, and headed for home.

Jane crinkled the lunch sack and peered inside at the brown bulbs. "Mommy, tell me story," she said. In Holly's former life, her life before she knew all the characters on *Blue's Clues* and wore stretch marks from hip to hip, she had spent a year in graduate school teaching freshman composition and preparing to write a thesis on folklore and urban legend. Coming up with strange, unique stories to tell her daughter was one of the only links to her past, and she relished it.

But as she looked at the long stretch of Boones Ferry ahead, her hands gripping the steering wheel at ten and two o'clock, the only story that kept running through her head was a grotesque one, completely inappropriate for her daughter's ears. It was the old story of the organ thief, one she'd studied in hundreds of different forms. Her favorite version began with candlelight and a romantic evening at a naive woman's apartment, and ended with the woman waking in a bathtub full of ice, a lipstick message scribbled hastily on the bathroom mirror: DON'T MOVE, CALL 911. The woman feels a pain in her back and reaches behind her to find a bloody wound. Her kidney had been harvested, sold on the black market for organ donation.

Holly could have imagined herself a part of some silly urban legend, except there was no bloody wound, no lipstick on a bathroom mirror, no second-hand narrator with her face in a flashlight to swear this happened to a "friend of a friend." Jane was still whining for a story when they pulled into the driveway, but by the time Holly had unbuckled her five-point harness and gathered the flower bulbs with their flaking skins from her lap she let it go.

Kevin came home while she and Jane were planting. They packed pebbles tightly into the little pots until each of the bulbs was buried in whiteness. He kissed them both, grabbed an apple from the fruit basket, and asked what they'd done that day. Before Holly could answer, Jane yelled "kidney doctor!" and laughed, then popped a white rock into her mouth.

So Holly told her husband, in the best way she knew how, that she seemed to have misplaced a vital organ. From their blankets of white gravel, the green tips of the bulbs stared up at them like eyes.

Her Body: A Well-Oiled Machine

Everyone facing kidney disease has questions and concerns about their future; you are not alone! Holly stood at her kitchen sink, washing dishes, thinking about the words she'd read on a website a few minutes earlier. The problem was, though, that she wasn't facing kidney disease. Dr. Whitney and his colleagues could find nothing to explain what had happened to her kidney. Her urine output was fine, there was no protein in the samples she handed them in paper cups. No pain in her side, nothing unusual at all.

She and her husband had left Jane with her mother and met with Dr. Whitney's whole team earlier in the day. They'd all tried to convince her she would be better off if they admitted her to the hospital to keep a closer eye on her condition, but she had refused. She felt fine, after all, not a stitch out of place. Dr. Whitney had sighed and then smiled, while one of his colleagues sat taking digital photographs of her and of her x-rays on the light box.

She'd made herself a pledge after Jane was born that she would avoid hospitals at all costs. The birth itself went smoothly enough, but shortly after delivery, Jane started having trouble breathing. It was the beginning of a four-week roller-coaster ride, with Jane in the ICU at Emmanuel Children's, tubes coming from every angle of her body. She looked to Holly like a sick little frog in a science lab, her sallow skin taut and thin under the warming lights of her isolette. Holly spent hour after hour stroking Jane's little hand and pouring breastmilk through a tube in her tiny stomach, or staring at her baby while she held a noisy pump to her rock-hard breasts. By the time Jane was released, she and Kevin had already vowed not to have any more children. They'd already spent a lifetime's worth of worry and heartache on a four-week-old child, and knew they couldn't do it again. She was the one to make the appointment for Kevin's vasectomy, and she never had second thoughts about it, even when he came home slightly loopy on codeine with a small ice pack between his legs.

She couldn't do that to either her husband or her daughter. She didn't want them to have to worry while she lay in a hospital bed having test after test done. She didn't want to have to endure another moment of that sterile, souring hospital smell. She finished the last dish and then filled a tall glass with water from the tap. While the cold liquid ran down her throat, she envisioned it making its way through the various clogs of her body until it reached her one remaining kidney and then was processed through her as urine. She imagined her body a well-oiled machine, her remaining kidney taking up the slack for its missing partner without even the slightest hitch.

Nothingness in the Perfect Shape of a Soup Bean

The paperwhites had grown to four-inch stalks when her other kidney vanished. It was a Tuesday again. Jane woke Holly early in the morning by jumping on the end of her bed and begging for a bowl of hot oatmeal. Holly opened her eyes, looked at her daughter with her curly blond hair and sleep-filled lashes, and promptly started sobbing. She cried while she filled the saucepan with water and dumped in a cup of oatmeal; she cried while she turned the television to Elmo and his bored-looking fish named Dorothy; she cried while she undressed to step into the shower. Jane followed her from room to room, occasionally offering one of her favorite toys or a hug, which only made Holly cry harder. The grief was from somewhere in her body she couldn't name. It was a liquid grief, pulsing through her very veins.

She called Dr. Whitney, and an ultrasound that afternoon confirmed what Holly already knew—that where there was once a vital organ there was only black nothingness in the perfect shape of a soup bean.

She'd sat in his office, surrounded by every one of the nephrologists in the building, with some pathologists and surgeons thrown into the mix for good measure, wearing nothing but a chilly paper gown. They asked her to drink water from quart bottles and then empty her bladder. They poked and prodded on her back and sides. While Kevin sat in the waiting room holding Jane, they ran a gel-covered ultrasound wand over Holly's stomach, her thighs, her chest just above her breasts, convinced they'd find the wayward organs somewhere. One of the younger doctors, a woman with short blond hair, kept looking at Holly accusingly and saying, "It's not medically possible," as if Holly had faked the whole thing.

That night, Kevin made Holly stay in bed while he thawed one of the tuna casseroles from the freezer. She could hear him making calls to her family, talking in a hushed voice as if the slightest disturbance would alert her body to the grim reality that it should not be working, that she shouldn't be living at all, and after a few final beats of her heart (for drama) she'd be gone. He brought her the casserole on a bed tray with a cup of hot coffee.

"It's either Mother's Day or I'm on the brink of death," she teased him. "Which is it?"

Kevin looked stunned. "This isn't funny," he said. "I might lose you."

"Honey, if I were on the brink, I'd know it. This is silly." Kevin left the room then, and Jane looked at her mother.

"Mommy sick?"

"Nah."

"What did doctor do?" Holly thought about the endless ultrasound of every part of her body, the well-dressed doctors on a sonographic search and rescue mission for her lost organs. She tried to explain to Jane that the doctors were taking pictures of the inside of her body, and when she could tell her daughter still didn't quite seem to get it, she grabbed Jane's baby book from the cupboard underneath the television. There, on the first page, were the ultrasound photos of Jane as a fetus. In the first one, taken at ten weeks, Jane was just a little round mass the size of a kumquat, floating in a what looked like black fog, a bright spot in her middle to indicate a beating heart. The next ultrasound was done at twenty weeks, and in this Jane looked almost human, arms, legs, and toes complete and in place.

Jane lost interest quickly and began dancing around the room on her tiptoes, pretending to be a ballerina. Holly watched her dance and then looked down at the photos in her hand. She could remember distinctly what she felt when she saw that beating heart on the ultrasound screen. She felt full of everything—full of wonderment, full of excitement, vulnerability. Full of life, with two hearts beating in her instead of just one. For a time she'd had more organs than usual, an extra tiny one to match each of her own. Sitting there with the fraying photos in her hand, her body emptying out instead of filling up, she thought she could almost imagine why someone would do it a second time.

Mr. Potato Head (an Explanation)

It was only a matter of days before the news cameras parked themselves at the base of their driveway. Holly ignored them for most of the week and refused to comment, which wasn't hard since her husband and mother wouldn't let her leave the bed except to make a daily trip to the hospital each morning to have blood drawn. When Kevin came home from work, she'd hear the reporters clamoring: "Is it true, sir, that your wife has no kidneys? What is her prognosis? Do you think she'd make a statement for us?"

It was surreal, seeing occasional glimpses of the front of her house on the nightly news. Her husband was blasé about it, assuring her it would pass and that she was just a "human interest" story; people, he would say, are drawn to anything out of the ordinary. Still, it was unnerving for Holly to see the sloppier aspects of their lives illuminated on television—her unmowed grass, her front door with the chipping green paint, Jane's muddy size-six boots lying slapdash on the front porch—all above the station's caption of choice, some variant of "Lake Oswego Miracle Woman Alive with No Working Kidneys." She moved her pots of paperwhites, each one just on the threshold of blooming, to the windowsill so there would at least be something lovely for the cameras.

And then the more negative attention kicked in. They started getting nasty notes from some of the neighbors on their street who were tired of the constant stream of reporters and cameras. On three separate nights, Holly woke to the sound of great thuds hitting the front of their house. She sent Kevin out to explore, and his report was that someone—teenagers, he suspected—had struck their garage door with large pieces of fruit and cans of kidney beans.

It wasn't long before Holly reached the point that she could no longer take the phone's constant ringing, be it caring inquiries from concerned friends or strangers wanting a good laugh or the inside scoop on Lake Oswego's Miracle Woman. She snatched the receiver from its cradle and dropped it onto the bedroom floor, watching it twist and dangle. When she looked up, Jane was watching her. Holly could tell that in her three-year-old way, Jane wondered what all the hubbub surrounding her mother was for. She must have wondered why her grandmother had come for an impromptu visit, spending the days flitting about the house cooking and cleaning while her mother stayed in bed in a rumpled nightgown. She must have wondered, Holly knew, why strangers showed up on the doorstep with huge cameras on their shoulders. She pulled her daughter into bed with her and Jane tucked her curly blond head under Holly's chin and laced her small fingers, sticky from the day's play and sliced oranges at lunch, through Holly's own.

"Mommy sick?" Jane asked. Holly hesitated. Technically, she knew, she probably was, but she had yet to feel anything other than that day-long sense of grief that accompanied each loss.

She answered, "Nah, not really." Jane looked up at her, disbelieving. "Think of me," Holly tried again, "like Mr. Potato Head."

Jane lifted her head and smiled. "Like I have Mr. Potato Head?"

"Yeah, just like the one you have. You know how he's all empty inside?"

"He keeps stuff in his bum."

Holly laughed. "Yeah, he's all hollow inside so you can put stuff in his bum. I'm kind of like that. It's just that everyone wants to know why I am so lucky to be like him and no one else is." Jane seemed to like this explanation. She tucked her head under Holly's chin again and they sat there until Jane fell asleep. It was something that hadn't happened in months. Jane was slowly cutting out her nap, most days, and to sleep she needed the perfect set of circumstances, the full routine: story, sippy cup of milk, stuffed platypus tucked under her right arm. Holly sat perfectly still, not wanting to wake her. She hadn't realized before how childlike Jane had become, and she smelled her hair, missing those moments when an infant Jane would surrender everything to her and sleep the day away on her shoulder.

When Jane awoke, Holly got out of bed, ignoring her mother's protests, dressed herself, and vowed to live her everyday, ordinary life again.

A Urine Sample, a Nobel Prize

Some of the theories, courtesy of those interviewed on KGW and KATU's late-night news: an expert at Oregon Health Sciences University thought it must be sonographic error, that for some reason the kidneys were there but not being seen. An older woman Holly recognized as a neighbor down the block whom she'd never met claimed the story must have been fabricated just to get attention. A new age–looking homeopathic doctor (complete with clichéd crystals around her neck) solemnly told the camera that "the human body has quirks and nuances we can't even begin to comprehend. Vital organs are vital only in that we can't comprehend living without them; obviously this woman has a strength of mind and energy we should all strive for." A man in his late forties, interviewed from his living room in Chicago, claimed to have been suffering from fatal kidney failure that was inexplicably cured just as Holly's kidneys checked out. "I'd like to thank her someday," he told the camera, the glimmer of a tear in the corner of his left eye.

None of this surprised her too much. Before she quit graduate school, she'd been researching a news story that smacked of urban legend: a technically brain-dead child, kept alive in her parents' home, who was said to have amazing powers to heal. Just being in her presence was enough, witnesses claimed, to induce miracles. Holly had searched newspapers from around the country to find similar stories, variations that would prove this legend was being circulated in many different forms, but she never found anything but the original story. Perhaps hers was a variation in and of itself.

Soon, she was receiving letters from people across the country, people who were sure she must have some sort of healing powers and were eager for just a moment of her time. The academic Holly wanted to laugh at the irony that she had become the central character in another legend, but the everyday Holly (the one who cooked macaroni and cheese out of a box and was proud of her ability to fold laundry and talk on the phone at the same time) found herself frozen to the core when these letters came, stunned that someone would think she was endowed with mystic powers when, after all, she couldn't even locate her own kidneys and most days she felt accomplished if she wrestled her three-year-old out of her pajamas and into real clothes by suppertime.

It was this Holly who had a grand epiphany on Dr. Whitney's office toilet. It happened like this: she was holding a plastic cup between her knees, praying that the stream of urine would make it cleanly into its target and miss her fingers altogether. Jane was on the floor in front of her, playing two flipped-over specimen cups as if they were drums. When the cup was full, Holly wiped herself clean and held the yellow liquid in front of her. It was the latest in a long series of almost daily samples she'd given them, along with vial after vial of her blood, all of which continued to show the same result: that her body continued to function as if her kidneys still lived there. It occurred to her, sitting on that toilet, that she couldn't afford to give any more. How much could she empty out, after all? All that blood, all that urine, two vital organs? At this rate, there would be nothing left. She dumped the urine into the toilet, pulled up her pants, flushed, and told Jane to get up off the floor. Dr. Whitney didn't seem surprised when she told him she was through being checked and monitored unless something else noticeable happened to her, but he did get her to agree to sitting in on a press conference later that week at the hospital to "get them off our backs."

The press conference was just as she imagined it would be: She and Kevin sat before a long wooden table, flanked on either side by doctors. An array of microphones, all different shapes and sizes with colorful station logos at their bases, stared up at them. There were rows of bright lights and people holding cameras; there were reporters scribbling in tiny notebooks the way they did in movies. Watching from the sidelines was Holly's mother, holding Jane and trying her best to keep the child from running amok among all the people and equipment. Kevin said little during the conference, but he sipped from his water nervously and squeezed Holly's hand when she repeatedly assured the cameras that she felt just fine, nothing out of place. Then they focused on the doctors, who would only say that they were researching some leads (Holly thought this made her body seem like a crime scene, her missing kidneys a case of foul play needing solving). A reporter from Channel 8 wearing blue jeans and a red sweater vest raised his pen.

"Isn't it true, Dr. Whitney, that a viable explanation as to why Mrs. Martino is still alive, if published in the right venue, could make you a shoo-in for a Nobel Prize?"

Dr. Whitney was smiling, as usual. "I suppose so, yes." Then he added, "But my primary objective is to help my patient."

That night, Holly dreamed that she caught Dr. Whitney leaving her bedroom with a bloody knife in a Ziploc freezer bag and her kidneys in an Igloo cooler, the words "Nobel Prize" written in lipstick on her mirror.

There Were Reminders, of Course

The next month was mostly uneventful, and any outsider unaware of Holly's strange situation would never know they were a family touched by miracles, that Holly herself was living a medical impossibility. She ran Jane to preschool in the mornings and picked her up just before lunch. She watched the food network and tried new recipes for dinner. She went to the salon and had the golden highlights in her hair redone. She and Kevin hired a babysitter and went out to eat a couple of times, sometimes making love when they arrived home, sometimes flipping on the television instead and watching the nightly news until Jay Leno came on, an unspoken relief between them that it was no longer their own front door they saw plastered across the screen.

There were reminders, of course. On a Wednesday morning, the sky overcast and threatening snow, Holly dropped Jane off at the preschool and then pulled into her driveway to notice a woman sitting on her doorstep. The woman was in her late twenties, her hair cut short and well coiffed. Holly thought she was dressed as if she had money, as if she were a woman with hardly a care in the world. When she saw Holly step out of the car, she stood and dusted off her skirt, a serious expression on her face. She touched her hair nervously just above the ears.

"You're Holly Martino," she said. Holly nodded her head and walked toward her door. The woman continued, "I hope you can help me."

Holly said, "I don't think so." Something quick like fear pulsed through her, and her only thought was to get inside her house, close the door, forget this woman had come. Even after the woman grabbed her by the arm and pleaded with Holly, told her that she'd lost both ovaries to cancer when she was a teenager and now wanted a child, Holly could only conjure fear and loathing when she knew she should find sympathy instead.

She said, "I'm not a healer."

The woman said, "But you're alive despite missing something vital, too."

And Holly: "I'm not a healer."

Holly pushed her way inside and closed the door behind her, her hands trembling. A nausea rose in her stomach and she shook it off by closing her eyes. She felt terrible for abandoning the woman on her doorstep, but what was the alternative? Should she have pronounced the woman healed, right then and there in front of her chipping green door, this woman she'd never seen, this woman she knew she had no power to help? Should she have placed her palm quickly against the woman's forehead and watched her fall backward the way they did on evangelical television specials, caught full force with the power of healing? Would she have walked past Holly's unmowed grass and into the street, sure with the knowledge of new life in her womb?

After a few minutes of silence had passed, Holly pulled the curtain tentatively from the living room window to assure the woman had left. She noticed her paperwhites sitting on the sill, green stalks too tall to stand straight any longer in their pots, the blossoms now brown and flaky. She had missed their blooming entirely.

Five Perfect Points

So this is what dying is like, Holly thought when she woke two weeks later, sure her time had come. Pain coursed through her abdomen and down her groin as if someone were holding a sharp instrument by its hilt and driving it through her. From all she'd learned of kidneys throughout her ordeal, she knew this must be her urethras and ureters shutting down, drying up, finally waking this cold Wednesday morning to the fact that they had no power sources to back them up any longer. She rose from bed, and with her rose a nausea that she could only ascribe to her fear of dying, now that her day had come. Or it could be her body looking to complete its emptying out.

What should she do, on her last day, in her last hours? The question puzzled her a bit. She pulled her bathrobe around herself and decided against a shower—there wasn't time, and she knew they'd take great pains to clean her after she was gone, coif her hair a final time, dress her in her finest. She bent over from another stab of pain in her groin and then walked to Jane's room, where Jane lay in the middle of the bed in her Minnie Mouse nightgown, breathing with her mouth open, her covers strewn onto the floor. Holly caught a sob in her throat. Far worse than the fear that she would lose Jane, really, was this one: the fear that Jane would lose her. What does that do to a child? How would she fare?

Before Jane woke that morning, Holly made three casseroles and placed them in the freezer, knowing full well that if this indeed was the end, her family would be flooded with more food than it would know what to do with. She scrubbed down the kitchen counters and the bathroom sink, knowing full well, too, that her mother would repeat the task the moment she heard the news, not knowing what else to do for Kevin and Jane. After Jane woke, she stroked her hair lightly and let her sit in front of *Sesame Street* while she continued her preparations: She vacuumed every floor in the house. She took a toothbrush to the top of her white baseboard moldings and scrubbed away the dirt. She pulled everything from the hall closet and threw half of it away. She did the same with the closet in her bedroom, pushing things aside, throwing things out, making room. She put a load of laundry in the wash and then threw up in the toilet. Afterward, she sat on the floor of the bathroom flooded with the relief that can come only in such a moment, wondering if this threshold on whose edge she tottered really did belong to death.

When she called Dr. Whitney, awed that they patched her through directly to the doctor instead of making her wade through oceans of receptionists and advice nurses, he told her he wanted to see her immediately, and asked if she wanted an ambulance sent out. Holly declined the offer but loaded her daughter, still in her nightgown, into the car and set out toward the medical building adjacent to St. Vincent's where she'd spent so many hours over the past few months. She still felt the pangs in her groin, the unsettled something in her stomach, but her mood was changing inexplicably from a generalized doom to a sort of excitement. Jane sang in the backseat while Holly waited impatiently at red lights and forced herself to slow down in school zones.

When she parked in front of the building, she stepped from the car and took a look at her reflection in its window. She'd never even combed her hair that morning, and it hung in oily hanks around her face. She fished through her glove compartment until she found an old newspaper rubber band and used it to form a careful ponytail in the back of her head. By this time, Jane had grown restless and was pulling at the straps of her car seat, begging for release. Holly unbuckled her daughter, looked up at the building looming in front of them, reached for her purse only to realize she hadn't thought to grab it on her way out, and headed inside.

She regretted that she'd called the minute she found herself on the hard table again with cold ultrasound jelly spread over her back and sides. While they ran the wand over her body, she imagined the stuff spread on a sandwich with peanut butter. She chuckled a bit at that, watching Jane busy with a coloring book on the floor beneath her. She closed her eyes.

"Well, I don't see your kidneys," Dr. Whitney said. She didn't open her eyes, but she could hear the trademark smile that came at the end of his sentence. "Let's take a look at your ureters and bladder. The pain is in your groin, you say?" He squirted more of the jelly on her stomach and pushed down with the wand, searching for the right angle, she knew, to see what he needed to. After a few moments of silence, he said, "Well, Mrs. Martino, you appear to be pregnant."

She kept her eyes closed, because behind them she could suddenly see what the doctor must be seeing on the screen: a shape, a pulse, a tiny, beating ball of life. It was so clear to her—why hadn't she seen it earlier? She didn't open her eyes even as Dr. Whitney went over the impossibility of a baby being carried to term, the necessary role of the kidneys in a pregnancy. She stared at that pulse behind her eyelids and wanted to laugh at how accurate she'd been with Jane: she was like a Mr. Potato Head, emptying out, making room for all the extras that came with this second child. Those blank, empty spaces her kidneys once filled were safe little pockets, like the cheeks of a chipmunk, that would hold the worries, the frustration, the unknowing.

She left the office quickly and lifted Jane into her car seat, snapping and buckling in all the necessary places. She wished on the drive home that she'd taken the name of the childless woman who showed up on her doorstep, if only to tell her that making room isn't a bad thing, and it all comes out, somehow, in the end. In her rearview mirror, Holly saw that Jane's eyelids had begun to droop, her nightgown bunched up under the buckle between her thighs, secured from whatever might come by the five perfect points of her harness: one point between her legs, two points on either side of her small little thighs, and from above her the last two points, looking down on their charge—her daughter's bony shoulders, slumped in sleep.

Raccoons

Police destroyed a large sick raccoon reported
in the backyard of a home in the 5300 block
of Lakeview Boulevard.

—*Lake Oswego Review* police blotter

TUESDAY MORNING, I wake with my husband's hand on my sleeping shoulder, his grip firm. When he sees me open my eyes, he moves wordlessly away from the bed and turns the volume up on the television. I draw the matted bangs away from my face in time to see what looks like an airplane fly straight into a skyscraper and not come out the other side.

"Holy hell," Carl says. And then, "That's the second one."

It's an image we see over and over again—the planes flying in, the towers crumbling, all surreally without noise—for the next hour, until Abby runs into the room and hoists herself over the side of our bed. I instinctively wrap my arms around her six-year-old body, but my eyes don't leave the television. I see Carl almost leap across the bed to find the remote control and turn the television off. The picture implodes from the outside in, shrinks until the falling towers are no more than a dot in the center of the screen, then nothing. Outside, I hear the rain where it drops a cadence on our roof.

As if this were any other ordinary morning, Abby yawns and shuffles her feet in restless circles atop the bedspread. "Mom," she says, "can I watch a video?"

"No time," I say, looking at the clock. "Let's get you dressed."

Abby moans. Our cat, Artemis, walks onto Abby's stomach and rubs her furry cheek against Abby's pajamas. Abby says, "Can I stay home today?"

It's a script we've followed every weekday morning in the three weeks since we moved to this new place. What follows should be my telling Abby that she and her brother will learn to make friends in Lake Oswego, that they'll probably like their new school every bit as much as their old one, that dads change jobs all the time and moving is never the end of the world. But today, all I can see in my head are commercial jets flying haphazardly in the sky above us, aiming for who knows what next, and I, too, yearn for the familiar. I tell her to go wake her brother just as Carl cinches the knot in his tie and kisses us good-bye. His eyes meet mine just before he leaves for work, and in them I see all the anxiety I'm feeling about what we just watched unfold on television.

Abby leaves the room, and I quickly turn the television back on, perversely hungry for just another glimpse. I know it will take awhile for her to rouse Isaac, and she'll return to my room soon, frustrated by her older brother. Isaac was up late last night waiting for the only thing that's brought him joy in our new move: the two raccoons that sneak up on our back deck at just after ten o'clock every night. They're so used to people that they let Isaac sit on the other side of the deck as long as he doesn't approach them. He watches while they eat the snacks he's left them, bringing their two paws up to their mouths and nibbling, humanlike. It goes against my better mother-judgment to let a ten-year-old sit outside with potentially dangerous animals, to let him stay up so late, even. But I am part of the enemy in this move, and I need all the points I can get.

I turn off the TV again as I hear Abby's feet, heavy in her run down the hallway, and Katie Couric's soothing voice echoes in a strange place between my ears, some physical place inside my skull, and settles there like a heavy stone.

* * *

By the time Abby and Isaac are ready to be picked up from school, I've had my fill of the news. I keep the radio off on my way to the school, but the silence is unnerving; I want my children bickering in the backseat so I can try to convince myself that our lives are the same today as they were yesterday. The drive to Bryant Elementary is a short one, and it always catches me off guard. In the tiny coastal town of our previous life, the drive to the kids' school was three times as long—just long enough to clear my head before that final bell rang, before I joined the swarm of mothers waiting for the clamor of children into vehicles. If it had been a particularly rough day, and I left the house early enough, I would take the long route, winding the car along the logging skidroads that connected our house with the rest of the town.

I'd give anything for those empty logging roads today, instead of street after street of suburban paradise: manicured lawns, large Lake Oswego McMansions with brick fronts and hedges squared just so, each street thick with a wash of gray because of today's rain. We're in that strange transitional time between seasons; just yesterday it was eighty degrees and hot, and this town looked like midsummer instead of early fall.

I turn into the parking lot at Bryant and am lucky to find an empty space along the curb. I let the car idle as I step outside and wait for Abby and Isaac, holding a spare sweatshirt over my head to protect myself from the rain. I can tell by the calm sense of order outside the building that the final bell has yet to ring. Mothers like me wait near the front doors or by the curb in a line of mini-vans and sport utility vehicles. When the bell rings, Isaac's class comes out first, and I can tell by the way he's running toward the car that he has seen me but is pretending not to have, that he wants to just fold himself into the passenger side of our car and attract no notice to the fact that he has a mother, that his life can be traced to some origin.

"Whoa, Buddy," I say, "slow down." He kicks his feet into the pavement and starts walking deliberately slowly now, just to annoy me, his jacket dangling from his right hand and dragging along the damp ground as he walks. I catch up to him and lift his jacket from the ground, folding it around his arm so it won't drag.

Under his breath, he says, "Knock it off, Mom!" His teeth are clenched. He continues his slow pace, and soon Abby is walking just behind him, which catches me off guard because I never saw her come through the front doors. She says hi to her brother, but he ignores her and picks up his pace, pushing his way through the crowd of children making a run for freedom through the rain.

Abby catches my eye and screams when she sees I'm watch-ing, tells me that Isaac is *totally* being a *jerk*. She watches my face to see if she's done the job, if he'll get a talking to as soon as we get in the car. She's holding something behind her back, and I play her game, pretend not to notice.

I say, "Don't worry about your brother, Abbs. School okay?"

"Yeah," she tells me. "Mrs. Radovich gave me *this*." She brings her hand from behind her back and shows me a tiny plant in a plastic pot, just a small bean shoot really, growing about an inch above the soil. I act enthusiastic as she tells me that her class made beans sprout in science and the teacher chose her to bring one home. Her face is smug and she lifts her skirt to scratch her thigh. It's the same pleated skirt she wore yesterday, a bright pink number from Gap Kids. In the same instant, I see Isaac walk toward the car, his hair dripping with rain, and slip just as he reaches for the door handle.

"Shit," he mutters under his breath as he picks himself up off the ground.

Abby screams, "I heard that!"

"Isaac!" I say. Just his name. I can't think of anything else; this is new territory. Isaac starts giggling nervously as he pulls his seatbelt across his shoulder.

"Mooom, I *heard* that!" Abby cries again, slapping her hands against her skirt.

"Abby! Don't whine. I'll talk to your brother when we get home," I say, loudly and firmly enough that I know Isaac is worried, though he's trying hard not to show it. I see him in my rearview mirror as he lifts his head and stares out the window He has Carl's nose, a small bump at its bridge as if a tiny seed is sitting dormant under his skin.

He says, "Did you see the planes crash, Mom?"

Why am I caught off guard? I should have anticipated this, that the teachers would talk to the kids at school about what happened this morning across the country.

"Yeah, I saw them," I say.

"Was it cool?" he asks, and then, "What did it look like?"

Abby says, "Some kids at recess said there were dead bodies everywhere."

I'm silent. Here it is: my chance to practice what I think I know about parenting, my pivotal moment as a mother when I can direct their emotions, help them know what to think, that everything will be okay, that life will be worth living. But all I can muster is this silence. I wish I could stop the car and hold them to me, shrink them back to the size they were just a few years ago when I could tuck their little bodies under my chin easily and swiftly. I feel a tightening in my stomach, and wish I could hang both my children permanently from my underside like a mother gorilla, hidden under the folds of my own body.

Behind me, Abby holds her little seedling extended in front of her with both hands. She does this the whole ride home. The plant is a guide, a beacon, pushing us toward the inevitable future.

* * *

Isaac goes straight to the back deck when we get home, his hood pulled up against the rain. When he comes back inside, it's to ask where the cat food and peanut butter are. He tells me he found a book about raccoons in the school library today, and he wants to set some things out that Scooter and Lucky will like.

"Scooter and Lucky?" I ask.

Abby looks at me as if I am an idiot. "The *raccoons*, mom. Isaac named them."

"Isaac, they aren't pets, you know," I start, but he's already rummaging through the pantry in search of peanut butter.

He says, "I hate this new house. I can't find anything."

I say, "I can't either. We'll figure it out."

He's spreading the peanut butter on the deck and sprinkling the cat food on the benches when the doorbell rings. It startles all three of us; we haven't had many visitors in the three weeks since we moved in, and we aren't accustomed to the shrill sound. I answer the door with Abby at my heels, and I recognize one of the neighborhood boys from Isaac's class. I've seen him playing basketball in his driveway with his older brothers.

He asks, "Is Isaac here?"

"Sure," I answer. "It's Harrison, right?" The boy nods. I usher him to the back deck and try not to look as if I'm listening when Harrison asks Isaac if he can play for awhile. Isaac shrugs his shoulders, ever the cool character, and says, "Guess so." Within minutes, the boys have disappeared into Isaac's bedroom and Abby follows them down the hall. I stand in the middle of my new living room, surrounded by boxes yet to be unpacked, unsure of what to do. I want to kick my feet up on the coffee table and relax, but I know that if I turn on the television the only thing I'll find will be images of people covered with ashes, firefighters digging through rubble, that little running text line at the bottom of the screen flashing the latest death toll. I could finish the business of moving by sorting through some of these boxes and putting our household goods in their respective places, but it seems like such a small, trivial act in the light of the real tragedy people are facing on the other side of the country.

It doesn't take long before I decide to see what the children are up to. Even in my most anxious moments, watching the ease of their play is always a magnificent cure, a reminder that life isn't nearly as complex as I make it out to be. Except this time, when I get to Isaac's room, Abby, Isaac, and the neighborhood kid have set up an elaborate game that takes the whole span of the bedroom. I stand in the hallway, just outside the open door, in an attempt to stay out of their line of sight.

Abby must have coerced them somehow into a strange game of house. She's got a scarf draped elegantly around her shoulders and is walking in circles with my dust wand hanging loosely from her right hand. She's got her doll, Marianne, the one whose eyes open and close if you tilt her head, in the cat's kennel as if it's some sort of cradle. Isaac and his new friend whisper something back and forth.

"Isaac." She feigns what sounds like an attempt at an English accent. "You and your brother need to watch the baby while I run to get groceries. Okay, *darling?*"

The boys hardly move from their end of the encampment. In what Abby must have set up as their bedrooms (a small space in the corner partitioned off with leftover moving boxes), they've arranged all sorts of weapons of war: water guns, light sabers, and Isaac's Spiderman action figures all litter the hardwood floor as if some sort of barricade from whatever Abby has planned.

Abby's patience is running out. "Well? *Isaac*, you promised you'd *play.*"

"Okay already. Yeah, fine. Go to the grocery store."

Abby picks up a small scrap of my fabric from the top of a box as if it's a memo pad and pretends to write on it. "This is the number where I'll be. Feed the baby in ten minutes." She opens the door of the Kitty Kab and pulls baby Marianne out through the narrow opening, careful to keep her head tilted back so that her eyes stay closed, and hands her to Isaac. With a flourish, she tosses the end of her scarf over her shoulder and disappears into the closet. I can see her peeking through the closet door to make sure the boys are playing their parts. Isaac picks up a water gun and starts blasting Marianne. Before Abby can leap out from her hiding place, the doll's dress (pink cotton batiste, striped) is dripping with water, and he's holding her upright by her squishy middle, her eyes open wide.

"MOM!" She calls for me. I'm caught. I step into the room.

I say, in as stern a voice as I can muster, "Isaac, if you aren't going to play right then you and your friend need to play a different game."

Abby whines, "But Mom! They *promised!*"

I look straight at her. "Hon, maybe the boys want to play something else." She ignores me. She waits until Isaac puts the gun down, then picks the feather dusting wand from the floor where she dropped it when she ran into the room and retreats back to her hiding place.

What comes next happens so fast that even I can't stop it. I've barely turned around when I hear Abby scream so loudly that I jump. Abby starts running at the boys, and Harrison is laughing out loud. In his right hand is Marianne's arm, severed from her body, and in his left is a pocket knife with a red handle, its blade long and rusted. Next to him, Isaac stands unmoving with a look of horror on his face. He doesn't take his eyes off the boy's hands, even to look at his sister, who by now is crying and grabbing at my arms.

Harrison's smile fails when I walk toward him.

I say, "Give me that thing."

He hands me Marianne's arm, the fibers of her nylon arm already fraying where they've been cut.

"The knife." I'm hoping the look on my face is as serious and commanding as I'd like it to be, that it doesn't betray how jelly-like and vulnerable my entire body feels. That it isn't clear to either of my children how frightened I am of this ten-year-old child in front of me. Abby starts crying louder, so I pick her up and settle her onto my hip, stroke her hair with my free hand. Harrison hands me the knife and doesn't say a word. He looks at Isaac and laughs, then says something about going home and leaves the room. When I hear the front door close, I release my breath and feel my legs shaking.

I tell Isaac to go to my bedroom and shut the door. "You can take Artemis with you, all right?" I add, because I'm not sure if I should be punishing him or soothing him. He hefts the cat into his arms and drapes her over his shoulder. As he walks off toward my room, Artemis looks at me with playful eyes, both of her paws hanging down his back, repeatedly gripping at his shirt with the claws she thinks are still there.

Abby pushes away from me and plops her small body onto the wood floor, then recoils against the feel of it on her bare legs. She pulls her knees inside her skirt and kneels on the fabric pleats, protected from the chill. "I want a snack," she says matter-of-factly, then remembers she is supposed to be upset and throws in a few sniffles to keep my sympathy.

I ask, "Would you like some crackers?"

She ignores my question. Instead, she says, "How come Isaac has a friend already and I don't?" It's this, more than the doll, that bothers her. As genuinely as I can, I reassure her that she will have friends of her own sooner than she thinks.

"I don't want a snack," she changes her mind, wiping her tears on her sleeve. "I want to play outside."

"Honey," I say, "it's raining."

Abby says, "I want to play *outside*." I nod my head in acquiescence, and she unwraps her legs methodically from the blue cotton pleats of her skirt as if opening a new and fragile gift, and then jumps to a stand, propelled to her feet by a hidden spring. She runs to her bedroom to grab her coat.

While I wait for her, I stick my head into my bedroom to check on Isaac. He's got the television on, and he doesn't even take his eyes from the screen when he hears me enter the room. He's watching a scene from outside a New York City hospital, where a crowd of people are holding pictures of their loved ones, asking if anyone has seen them.

"Did you see it?" I ask him. He nods his head and turns to me slowly. I look closely at his face. "Pretty scary, huh?" His eyes go blank and he shrugs, turning back to the television. He doesn't argue when I tell him I think he should maybe put a video in, that I don't want him watching any more of the news. But I linger an extra couple of seconds before I enforce the switch, because I'm curious myself what has unfolded since I last caught the news. Has something else been attacked? Some other tragedy unfolded? I think of Carl in his downtown Portland office building, so different from the small space he worked in when he was an engineer for the big mills. I think about the women in New York whose husbands won't be coming home tonight.

When Abby emerges from her bedroom, she's wearing a bright orange ski jacket from her closet, not the light rain slicker I sent her to school with this morning, but I say nothing. It's only for an afternoon that she'll look like she's swimming in an ocean of Tang, her arms tripled in size by the fluffy down hidden in the sleeves of the coat. She's bouncing the way she does when she gets excited, suddenly all smiles again. I don't give my kids enough credit for how quickly their world can go from chaos to bliss. It's a trait I wish I'd hung onto from my own childhood, though I'm unsure I ever had it in the first place. In the thin flesh of her hands, barely visible where they linger at the ends of her orange nylon sleeves, she's holding the potted seedling she brought home from school. I throw a scarf around my neck, the same one Abby wore just moments before, and open the door to the back deck for her.

We're a strange procession, Abby and I. I follow my daughter into the drizzle outside, her tiny green plant suspended before her, bending with the wind toward the soil from which it just sprang. Abby busies herself with digging in the moist bark dust to the right of the deck, pretending to plant the seedling in the earth. I watch her for a time, then just as I decide it's safe to go inside and leave her to her play, I hear a scratching on the underside of the deck. Artemis must have made an escape through the door while we came outside, and now she's taken cover from the elements underneath the wooden planks of the deck.

I descend the steps to the lawn, then walk to the side of the house where there is an opening to that murky place underneath the patio set. In the dark, I see two eyes flash in my direction, and it only takes a second to realize that I am looking not at the eyes of my cat, but one of Isaac's raccoons. As my eyes adjust to the dark, I see the thing lying against the house, its limbs limp with fatigue. I clap my hands and feign running toward it, but its face barely registers the threat. I step slowly in the direction of the raccoon, until I am less than five feet from its furry, masked face: it doesn't move. From this vantage, it's clear that the raccoon is not well—its eyes are red and runny, its fur glistening. I back out from the underside of the deck and tell Abby it's time to head inside.

I've heard stories about sick raccoons: spreading distemper, crazed with rabies. Today, though, in the great scheme of things (given the hijacking of planes, the destruction of massive buildings, the loss of thousands of human lives), should I really care? All it takes for me to finally call the city and report the sick animal is the picture of my son with this raccoon, his smooth, shaking palm outstretched in offering.

The police department tells me someone will be out soon. It's my first real exchange with officials from Lake Oswego—a city we chose because everybody told us how safe our kids would be, how much better the schools are than in the surrounding towns. I didn't expect neighborhood kids wielding knives, my son swearing within my earshot for the first time.

I didn't foresee having to pass along a death sentence for a creature my son loves.

*　*　*

By the time the officers arrive, Carl is home and we are halfway through dinner. When I hear the bell, I leave my family to their chili and baked potatoes and squeeze through the front door without having to open it all the way, in the hopes I can shield Isaac from the messy truth of what is about to happen. The officer who introduces herself as head of animal control is young and almost striking in her beauty. She is not, I think to myself, who I expected to come and dispose of sick raccoons. The male officer with her doesn't speak, but nods his head and whispers to the woman as I walk them around the back of the house and show them how to access the underside of the deck.

"Is it still there?" I ask.

The woman takes a few steps underneath, and then calls, "Yeah, he's sick all right." She backs out slowly and looks straight at me, smiling, "We'll take care of it from here." I start back around the house, but something makes me turn around again and pause: it's the same thing that makes me want to touch the power button on the television every time I walk past it, hoping against hope that it will show those planes again, barreling into the side of a wall of windows.

The young supermodel-turned-animal-control-officer gives a few words of guidance to her sidekick that I can't quite make out, and then I see him pull a gun from the black bag he has slung over his shoulder. He attaches a silencer to the front with a slow, deliberate screwing motion, and as he disappears under the house, the spell is broken and I turn around. In the seconds that I have paused, the rain has started coming down harder, and the waning sun makes the elements look all the more menacing. My feet are wet with the small rivers of rain that are running through the lawn.

A short walk to the front door suddenly feels like a major commitment, a dangerous journey. It will take some time for me to make the switch to Lake Oswego life, to this inland suburbia: I am used to our small coastal town, where too much rain often meant trouble. About five years ago, we got so much fall rain that a narrow stream formed between the Steelhead River on the other side of the main road and the creek in our neighbor's ravine. It ran right over the road in front of our house, blocking traffic for days. Carl and I brought Isaac outside to watch the water course over the dotted yellow line when he was smaller than Abby is now. He squealed in delight as whole branches, leaves, and other pieces of debris flew over the street in its wake. Every now and then, we could see a spawning salmon jump and flip across the road, trying to find its way upriver. It used its small fins and tail as propellers, and wriggled its way over the asphalt with short, quick flips of its body, following the water wherever it would lead.

I imagined I saw a look of sheer terror in the eyes of the salmon whenever they passed, their silver, scaly bodies glistening wet as they took a wrong turn, though of course I know they probably had no idea what was in store. I pictured them trapped and swimming in endless circles in our neighbor's creek once the water subsided, the one major event of their lives—for which they had trained since hatchlings—a massive failure.

It's an image that hasn't left me. I worry I'll see that look in my own children's eyes someday, their scales following the wrong waters. Helpless against the current. Too slippery for my grasp.

When I make it through the front door and shake the water from my hair, I can tell that the kids are done with dinner and Carl has the water running for Abby's bath. I hear them in the bathroom, negotiating over which toys she is allowed to bring into the mass of bubbles. I busy myself with the dinner dishes, scrubbing chili from the rims of our white Fiestaware. When I hear a loud thump from the back deck, I know it's the officers removing what is probably now a raccoon's lifeless body. I look up from the sink and that's when I notice Isaac: he's standing at the sliding glass door, watching.

I rush to the door in time to see the raccoon's charcoal fur as it is loaded into what looks like a burlap sack.

When I turn to Isaac, I expect to see tears on his face, but his eyes are dry and expressionless where they should be watery and red. He runs from the room before I can explain.

It's only now that I think to ask myself: who's in the bag—Scooter or Lucky?

*   *   *

I turn the lights out not long after we put the kids to bed. Carl crawls in next to me, the room dark, hours earlier than we usually sleep. I like the way this house feels: full, reasonable. Every living body accounted for, somewhere within. From behind, Carl clings to me and for the first time all day, I let myself go in fear. I wonder what it would have been like on those airplanes, settling in to read a magazine when a man stood up with a box knife in his hand. I wonder about the people who jumped from their office windows rather than wait to face the inevitable, about the things they must have said in the moments before the final plunge.

Carl nuzzles his head into my neck and starts nibbling on my ear, and when I feel him pressed against my leg, I consider it for a moment. But soon I push him back gently and moan a little to let him know I'm tired. I'm afraid all I'll be able to see the whole time we make love is Marianne's severed arm, the torn fabric at her shoulder, the neighbor kid's face as he stands so close to my son with the rusted blade in his palm, towering New York monuments collapsing as if they are made from playing cards.

But Carl is persistent, and soon we're shushing each other under a tangle of sheets, exploring each other's bodies piece by piece, knowing full well there will be no surprises in his flesh or mine. There are no hidden places we haven't already found. That's the comfort of marriage. When we're done, Carl is quickly asleep, but my senses are heightened and keenly alive. I listen to a silence in the house so profound that it unsettles me.

I get up to peek in on the kids and reassure myself that they're all right. I find Isaac and Abby sleeping in the same room. She does this a lot—instead of coming to our room, she'll sometimes choose to sleep on Isaac's floor when she's scared, pressed up against his bed. And though he won't admit it, I think sometimes Isaac asks her to, comforted by her sleeping presence just a few feet below him. Watching them this way used to make me feel as if the world had never been safer. Tonight, I think about the mothers of the men who forced their way into the cockpits. Did they once watch their sons sleep? Did they notice the same blankness in their ten-year-olds' eyes as I did in Isaac's, when confronted with grief, when facing sure tragedy?

Asleep, Abby and Isaac aren't competing for my attention or for my blame. Isaac is on his back, his hands under the covers and his mouth wide open. Abby is sleeping on her side, her sleeping bag twisted where her arm comes out to wrap around Artemis curled up next to her. I watch for the rise and fall of each of their covers, for the whistle of their sleeping breath to become audible over the heater that's just clicked on. I am amazed by their small shapes, that they ever once came from my body. It seems more likely they came from the earth itself, because each day they seem so solidly planted in universes of their own, outside of mine. Their bodies boast of their own private landscapes: Abby's feet, long and narrow for her height, are small hills where they arch; the lines of sweat that form on her forehead when she sleeps are small rivers unfit for a mother to travel on. Isaac's distinct shoulders and collar-bone are bearers of secret unmarked trails, hidden even from me.

And when they are awake: there are certain looks, certain glances they give me that put whole forests between our bodies. There are times when they call between them a truce, if only to share a meaningful look that says, This is a terrain Mom can't explore. Childhood has its own topography that I can't even begin to remember, a map of being where broken dolls and sick raccoons hurt far more than airplanes crashing into buildings. Watching them sleep, I am aware that the small tragedies of childhood smart every bit as much as the ones I am grieving over myself.

Above her pillow, Abby's gangly seedling is tipped to its side, and her doll is lying like a spent child. One of its arms is turned above its head and touches the wall. In the dark, I can barely make out the other one where it lies three feet away next to Isaac's head-board, its end jagged where it has been severed from its body. I sneak past Abby, tiptoeing in slippered feet so I don't wake them, and collect Marianne and her missing parts. By the time Abby wakes in the morning, her doll will be whole again, sewn with a thread so close to the color of its toy flesh that no one will be the wiser. When I sneak from the room and close the door behind me, no one stirs.

As if we are partners in a secret collusion, Marianne looks at me when I examine her again, standing in front of their closed door, her eyes winking at me whenever I move her too much. Her pink dress is wrinkled where it has dried from the earlier assault against her.

We're a strange procession, Marianne and I. We head toward the sewing room together, moving cautiously through the thick darkness of the house, bracing one another for the terrors of the unknown world. We pass the sliding glass door, and as I turn I see them: the surviving set of raccoon's eyes, glowing green in the moonlight. They look like that tiny dot, center screen, in the nanosecond before the television shuts off completely, and it seems that if I strain hard enough, I should be able to see the microscopic image of a commercial airliner in that glow, hurtling toward its inevitable end.

Rich Girls

Someone lit a fire in a boy's bathroom at Lake Oswego High School, 2501 Country Club, at about 3 pm March 20th.

Lake Oswego Review police blotter

SO I'M LYING on a hard table in a dimly lit room, in a part of the hospital I never knew existed, looking at some other man's hand packed in ice on a metal tray. Times like now I think, This thing has gotten out of control. And I lift my right hand, wiggle my fingers, say my farewells. It's been a good friend to me, this hand. Close to thirty years and counting. But that's medical science for you: no room for sappy talk, all business. And for the size of the check they'll cut me afterward, who can blame me?

I am a man who would do anything for his family.

This all started a few months ago, in the swanky French café on Boones Ferry Road, when my wife said she'd like to see the dessert menu. And I felt it again: a squeezing inside, like a vine winding from my stomach to my head, choking me from the inside out. It's hard to breathe like that. And the whole time she was talking to that waiter, the one with the pseudo-French accent, asking questions about which pastry was filled with what and did the ice cream thing come with nuts, and all I could see was a running tally inside my brain, adding up the cost of the movie and the meal and the six-dollars-an-hour babysitter, *cha-ching, cha-ching,* and then dessert too? Stephanie asked what I was having, because knowing would help her decide, and the vine squeezed harder and I told her: I'm full.

Stephanie gave me the look. Like she knew I'd kill for a crème brûlée but the only reason I held back was I was worried about the cost. She told the waiter we'd decided against dessert and then it was just the two of us. Stephanie and me and this fancy French tablecloth, yellow with poppies and olives twisting along the sides, and a little vase of flowers between our empty dinner plates. And just like that I felt like a prick. She said, "I thought we weren't worrying about money tonight." I begged her to order something, because I didn't want my old money fears to ruin the night, but she refused, because didn't I know it's not fun to eat dessert alone with your husband staring?

And then it was too late. My breath started coming in shorter waves, like my lungs were made of taffy. I promised her I'd order something, said, "Let's just not let this thing get out of control." But by then she'd grabbed her purse and said she'd meet me in the car. I paid the check with a credit card and by the time I got outside, it took two puffs on my inhaler to get my lungs settled.

Stephanie sat in the car, the radio turned up high. I could see her through the window, trying not to look mad. And there I was in the parking lot, watching the cars buzz past on Boones Ferry, hoping by the time we got home the kids would be in bed so I could relax with a beer or two. I imagined another man stepping into the car with my wife and laying his foot on the gas pedal, screeching off. The kind of man she should have married: veterinarian, lawyer, economics professor. The kind of guy who would never go into panic-induced asthma attacks over chocolate profiteroles and crème caramel. Except there was only me, so I got in the car and drove.

Which sort of explains why I was so moved when I saw the television commercial later in the night while I sipped my beer, Stephanie and the kids asleep in various rooms throughout the house. What happened was this: a man in a white coat with thick glasses and a comforting half-smile came onto the screen, hugging a clipboard to his chest. He looked right at me, I swear it, and I was only on my first beer so I know I wasn't even buzzed yet. He held a plastic lung and explained how crap gets all messed up in there when you have asthma. Then a number flashed across the screen and he promised up to a hundred bucks a day and free drugs for asthmatics to participate in a research study. At a hundred bucks a day, I knew my wife could order pork tenderloin or veal-stuffed-with-something off any menu in town without it sending me over the edge. I wrote the number on an old receipt in my wallet and called in the morning.

To get to the research office, I had to drive around the rear of the hospital and enter through a set of unmarked doors. It was six o'clock in the morning—still dark and cold, the only time I could make an appointment on account of the fact that I work all day for a living. I was the only one in the waiting room, it was so early, and this woman wearing jeans and a tee shirt, no white lab coat or anything, escorted me to an examination room and said the research assistant would be with me shortly. I waited.

I expected the guy from the commercial, the one with the thick glasses. But instead I got an older guy with gray streaks in the front of his hair, and he walked in and said, "We need to do a preliminary exam," and next thing I knew I was breathing into machines and having rubber hammers pounded into my knees. But the good news was I qualified for the study, which meant they kept my regular inhalers, and I took a pill a day instead. After that, I just needed to come in twice a week to have my breathing checked and each time I'd leave with a check written out to me, just like that.

Not a bad gig, all things considered. But the money didn't come easy. Some mornings, I'd start out my shift at the Volvo repair shop with what felt like a sponge lodged in my throat. If I had a big job that day—digging out a faulty carburetor, changing the brake pads on an old 240—it got so bad I'd have to lie down in the break room for a bit, underneath the table. I'd concentrate on nothing but pure, clean air. But then I'd remember the checks I picked up two mornings a week and I figured, what the hell? I could put up with some breathing annoyance for a little liquid income. Sometimes at night my girls would demand an extra bedtime story and I'd find it harder and harder to read the words out loud, like I'd just run the Hood to Coast, and I'd go to bed huffing and puffing like the big bad wolf.

In the meantime my oldest girl had started taking violin lessons, on account of our extra income. Years ago, I let my wife talk me into renting a house in Lake Oswego because of the better schools, which meant our kids had to work hard to keep up with the others. We were just two nannies and a Mercedes sport utility vehicle away from fitting in, now that Shelly played the violin. Except that hearing a seven-year-old practice "Turkey in the Straw" an hour a day was worse than any medical experiment they could perform on me. But Stephanie's convinced our kid is a musical genius, and I humor her.

I guess you could say it's the violin that got me into this hand business. Shelly had a recital on the final day of my asthma study.

I collected my last check in the morning and the old guy in the lab coat gave me my inhalers back, then I headed to work to completely overhaul the engine on a 740 wagon. I got off just in time to run home and shower before I met my wife and kids at the church that sits at the top of Mountain Park. We took a seat next to my best friend and his wife, who had come in from southeast Portland on account of the fact that they are Shelly's godparents. Trudie, my two-year-old, bounced and giggled on my lap, pulling on the buttons of my shirt, and I was aware of my wife at my left elbow, silent but content. After several puffs on my old inhaler throughout the day, my lungs felt new and clean again, like they'd been scrubbed sparkling with pipe cleaners.

And then Shelly came out from behind the stage. She had on a little purple dress my wife picked up at Hanna Andersson (I noticed the receipt on the counter, more than I would have spent on my own clothing). She drew that tiny instrument to her chin and she could have been somebody else's child, for as much as I recognized her. She glowed. Her little face reflected off the shiny brown wood of the miniature violin and when she moved her bow back and forth and her elbow stuck out just so, I couldn't help but feel a sense of pride, could I? When she finished playing, I took another puff to relieve the sluggishness of my lungs and my wife looked at me like, Couldn't you at least go outside to do that? And I decided that if I could find one good study, I could find another.

The graying lab coat man was really quite accommodating. He handed me a list of ongoing studies and a highlighter pen, and told me to mark any that struck my fancy. My hand shook, 'cause I couldn't really tell what any of them meant, but I picked the three with the highest dollar amounts in the right column and he smiled and I smiled and I thought of Shelly and her violin, my wife shopping at Hanna Andersson, and how we were all so happy we could burst.

 * * *

And now I'm waking up here, in this dimly lit room outfitted like a hospital except darker and smaller, and my head is fuzzy and I'm sick to my stomach and as I take stock of my body and its parts, I find I have somebody else's right hand. It's an altogether strange sensation. Aside from the line of stitches in a ring around my lower arm, my new fingers are slightly smaller than my old ones were. In the hours that follow, while I regain movement in my right hand, I find that when I go to pick something up—a glass of water, say—I clip my fingers together a smidgen too early because I am used to a little extra length, and I miss the glass altogether. When I raise my fingers to scratch my chin, I have to reach just a bit farther than I'm used to. I stand up straight in front of the full-length mirror attached to the back of the door and I can see that my left hand is a good two centimeters longer than my right.

 My researcher returns with the same smile on his face and a stack of paperwork for me to fill out. I'm nervous at first, on account of my right-handedness, but damned if I don't get used to the pen within my first two answers and soon I am writing like an old pro, pain-free, my penmanship crisp and perfect, better than it ever was. The research survey is involved but rather interesting. It has me draw my hand to my face and rotate my thumb in a full circle. It asks me to measure how far I can bend each finger, rate my pain level when I clap my hands together, when I bend the fingers back on my new hand and try to crack the knuckles. When I'm done, Mr. Lab Coat goes on and on about the exciting implications of quick, painless hand transplant while I step out of the blue paper gown and return to my work clothes, and then I'm standing outside, and I can tell by the light that it is almost dusk.

I've missed work and there will be some smoothing over to do. But I can get home in time that Stephanie won't bother to question me too much, and if she does, I've got a check for a thousand dollars in my wallet, and that should make her happy as hell.

I'll admit my new hand changes my way of looking at things, for a time. When I touch Trudie's cheek in the minutes before her eyes close and she goes to sleep, it's softer than it was before. I help Stephanie fix dinner, because with my new hand I can chop vegetables as fast as the chefs on television, where the celery and knife are flying so fast you can't tell what's happening until they lift their hands and there, on the cutting board, is a perfect pile of chopped food, shaped like a miniature pyramid. At work, I can close my eyes and put my hand on a transmission or an engine, and within seconds I can tell what kind of car it came from and what year, simply by the way each vibrates underneath my fingertips. And at night, in the bedroom, after the kids have gone to sleep, I am rediscovering my wife as if we've never been together before. I have to acquaint this new part of me with every space and crevice of her body, and it's as exciting for her as it is for me, which is something I can tell by the way she gasps and can't contain her noise when I touch her anywhere, just so, with the tips of the fingers of my new hand.

And it isn't until I'm sitting in a sports bar across the river in southeast Portland with my old high school buddies that my hand starts showing signs of wear. We've been here for over two hours and I'll admit it, yeah, that I'm starting to feel buzzed and so are they probably, and they start getting on my case, shit about me thinking I'm some sort of upper-class suburban mucky-muck instead of the Volvo mechanic I really am. And I think, have you seen my house? Have you seen our nine-hundred-square-foot rental with the dented moldings and orange shag carpeting—not the new, trendy kind, but the kind that was probably installed in nineteen-sixty-something? And I'm pissed, because I've told them we moved to Lake Oswego for the kids, but how can I expect them to understand? They don't have kids. I'm the one who knocked his girlfriend up a few years out of high school. And I go to reach for my beer and I see them: the fingers on my right hand, graying and wrinkled on their tips.

All in all it isn't a huge deal, at least not according to the guy in the lab—a new guy this time—even given the fact that the skin is now rubbery-gray and wrinkled down to the middle joint and continuing to spread. This new guy verifies what I already assumed, which is that they no longer have my hand. A reversal is out of the question, he says, which I should know, he says, because I signed the papers, right here, he says, which state expressly that I understood the procedure and risks and wished to go ahead anyway. He takes at least twenty digital pictures of the hand from different angles, then asks me to complete the same survey I filled out last time. This time, though, it isn't as easy. I can't move my thumb in a complete circle. It takes longer to bend each digit. I can hardly make a sound when I clap my hands together. And the pencil doesn't flow as easily in my hand; my writing looks like chicken scratch. But the check he hands me as I leave is the same size. And that's something. That gives me a bit of a lift.

Still, by the time I get home I can hardly breathe. My inhaler isn't even worth a damn. I can't help Stephanie bathe the kids and while she's tugging their nightgowns over their wet heads I can only sit by the window and gasp for air. Stephanie keeps looking at me as if I'm faking the whole thing, as if I am the most useless husband in the world. I can't help myself. I'm in bed before the kids are and I half expect to wake with blue lips, or not to wake at all, but when I open my eyes in the morning I can breathe again.

I get through the entire day without much problem, except for being slower than usual because of my failing hand, but I'm learning to accommodate with my left. Lesson: I am nothing if not adaptable. This guy I work with, a guy we call Slim and God knows what his real name is, he keeps looking at my hand and finally nods in my direction while he's on break and lighting a cigarette. I'm trying to pull a few spark plugs from a real pretty 780 Bertone, so I ignore him. But he says real loud across the garage, Hey, Jimmy, what the hell happened to your hand? And I pause for a second and can't think what to say. I shrug my shoulders and keep pulling on the plugs. Makes me wonder, though. Makes me wonder if I'm starting to look like Frankenstein's monster. I make some smart-ass remark like what my mom said was true, about what could happen if you jacked off too much, and that makes him laugh so hard he has to take the cig from his mouth.

Not that I can blame Slim for asking. Could I deny I would be curious in his place?

I find myself driving through Portland after work, the streets on the other side of the river where I used to cruise and hang out in high school and just after. Sometimes I'll take Shelly and Trudie with me to give Steph a break, and we get dinner at that barbeque joint off of Foster Road owned by one of my buddy's parents. It isn't a satisfying exercise. I come home stuck with the feeling that I will not be happy anywhere. The ribs are heavy in my stomach and I pass gas all night, so strong that my wife can't stand to be in the same room as me.

I've just had one of those nights the next time I'm scheduled for an early-morning visit at the lab. I wake with my stomach still touchy, and I can't bring myself to eat breakfast. I buckle my belt and tie my shoes with my left hand, because the fingers on my right will only bend a half inch, if that. By the time I leave my driveway that familiar taffy is stretching and pulling in my lungs, and I grab my inhaler from the glove compartment and I put it to my lips over and over. But the taffy takes hold and sticks and now I'm completely terrified, stomach sick, lungs tight, hand a mess of gray wrinkles. By the time I get into the waiting room I'm bent over, unable to get a breath. The woman behind the desk escorts me to my usual exam room and when the doctor walks in I recognize him. It's for real this time, the guy who brought me here, the one with the thick glasses from the television commercial. And it's like seeing an old friend, that's how much I want to trust him.

He smiles at me and shakes my hand, not looking down or noticing the unreal touch of my fingers, the weak, shaky grasp of my palm. He asks me to breathe into a little box to measure my lung capacity, which seems really stupid to me, given the fact I'm wheezing and probably blue all over. But I pass the test. This guy swears my lungs are fine. He says, "Explains why your inhaler isn't working." He says, "Mr. Nolan, this looks like your garden-variety anxiety attack." The way he says it strikes me as funny. As if there's exotic, tropical anxiety attacks. Desert-grade anxiety attacks. Forest-variety asthma attacks, the kind that run wild under thick canopies of trees. Leave it to me to have nothing but your good old garden variety.

But there's good news, 'cause as fate would have it they're running a high-paying study right now for sufferers of panic and anxiety. I fill out a stack of paperwork as best I can with my left hand and in return I get a bottle of pills to take when I feel an attack coming on. I do this for two weeks and then I'll qualify for the second phase of the study, which will require me to stay here for a day or two. So on my way out of the office I pop one of the pills without water, that's how small it is, roll it around under my tongue, and swallow the thing.

I'm almost to the garage when I feel a calm wash over me like none I've ever felt. I breathe in and the air travels for miles in and around my body, the most satisfying breaths I've ever taken, I swear to God. It lasts all day. It's as good a high as I've ever had. There are moments while I am at work that I feel like I'm behind the shed on the other side of the track field at my old high school with a bag of weed again, only better, calmer. I look at my hand and am filled with love for my new, faulty part, the anger long since gone. And at the end of the day, all I want to do is see my wife and kids, so much do I love them. I leave work early.

I'm almost home, in the heart of Lake Grove—only not our end, the end where the nice houses are. And it comes on as if someone has snapped and triggered it: the taffy lungs, the shaking, the panic. But it's different this time. Stronger. I fumble through my pockets with my good hand until I pull out the bottle of amazingly small pills and toss one under my tongue. And there it is again: instant calm. It's as if I can feel the stuff working its way into my brain, making little pathways of light and peace to leave me with this sense that all is right in the world. Instead of turning into my driveway, I keep driving around town, and all I can think is how much I love this place. Everything looks special and new, even the things that usually bother me most about Lake Oswego. The McMansions on the corner lots that used to be cute old cottages. Houses kept apart by enormous masses of waxy green-leafed hedges. The hanging flowerpots on the light posts, kept alive by the guy who jumps out of the back of a pickup every few feet in the evening to stick a long, stiff hose of water into them.

I come out on Country Club and take a left, driving toward the high school football field. Set back behind the field is the school itself, a building that looks more like a line of upscale row houses than a school. Before they remodeled the school, when it looked more like any of the old Portland high schools, mine included, we used to come here for football games and walk the track at halftime looking for trouble and making fun of the rich kids. During one game, a few of my buddies and I snuck away and used paper towels and lighter fluid to start a fire in the boys' bathroom. We bragged about it for weeks afterward, until one of the guys told us to shut the hell up, that was nothing, while we were lighting our little fire he was banging one of the rich cheerleaders in his Corsica. I remember picturing her: blond, leggy, her own cellular phone in a designer handbag, driving around town in a red Jeep Wrangler licensed to her. Damn.

I pop another pill and sit in the high school lot. How many hours had I spent wondering what that was like for him? I feel my brain expand, the pathways zip and surge, the peaceful swelling. It's all good. Shouldn't Shelly and Trudie get to be that girl? Why the hell not? They've got names fit for rich kids, perfect to be the head of a cheerleading squad, the kind of girl everyone else loves to hate. I smile as if it's ten years from now and Stephanie is the head mother of the team, Shelly and Trudie the two tiny girls on the top of the pyramid. From the stands, I wave as they cheer, my wrinkled, graying hand moving slowly through the air.

I turn the car around and head back across Country Club, into the mass of trees and houses that is Lake Grove. I take another pill because I want to give those lab guys something to find. I can guess what will come in phase two, when they go inside and see what the patterns look like inside my head, the road map that these pills have created with their little peaceful jolts of energy and calm. I can guess about the size of that check.

Shelly is practicing her violin in front of the window when I pull into the driveway. I scratch my cheek with my right hand, but I can't apply enough pressure with those wrinkled fingers to make it worth my while. I shut off the engine and stare at my oldest girl. The sight of that tiny little instrument on her shoulder fills me with desire—pure and strange. When that white-coated man with the thick glasses cracks my head, I want to have the prettiest brain on the block. I want it swelling and hot with calm, streaked with silver, like ribbons on a maypole. I want those rich girls to be mine. Stephanie, Shelly, Trudie. All three of them, with my last name, like they belong to me, like I'm the kind of guy who could give them anything.

IV

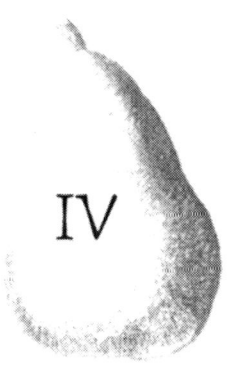

On the Lake

Of All the Insatiable
Human Urges

An "unknown hairy thing," found stuffed in a
trash can at New Waluga Park and described
as "heavy," was determined to be a stuffed
animal.

—Lake Oswego Review police blotter

JASMINE HAS ONLY slept with three men. Her high school boyfriend, in the last weeks of summer before they left for separate colleges. Her freshman mistake, a tall blond boy who claimed to be a poetry major, a boy she met at a party and never saw again. And then for the last fifteen years there has been Rick, her husband, the man she married her junior year of college. Rick has always been a slow, unadventurous lover, but Jasmine has never found reason to complain.

And now Rick's penis, the only one she has known intimately and not just in passing, is swollen almost beyond recognition, rendered useless by a cancer that has taken his prostate from the size of a walnut to the size, as Rick likes to say, of a small Volkswagen.

Jasmine and Rick don't speak much the entire drive up the hill to the Oregon Health and Sciences University Hospital. Dr. Craftsman had said in his phone message that he wanted to see them in person, which to Jasmine could only mean bad news. There is still a sprinkling of snow in patches along the roadside from the storm two weeks earlier, and their little Volvo sedan, with all its new car bells and whistles, seems to heave and resist the steep hill in this cold.

After parking the car in the visitor lot, after stopping for Rick to use the restroom (she waits fifteen minutes for him to pee, and he comes through the heavy door marked "MEN" looking pale and agitated), after giving his name to the receptionist and quickly being called into Exam Room 4, Dr. Craftsman sits on his small black stool, wheels himself closer to them, eyes on the manila chart in his lap, and says, "Mr. Duchane, the cancer is stage four."

While Rick and Dr. Craftsman discuss chemotherapy and other treatment options, Jasmine closes her eyes and envisions Phoenix in the early spring and their lives two years ago: flowers in bloom since January, a backyard swimming pool, a sweeping view from their kitchen window of Camelback Mountain. Working with watercolor on canvas in her outdoor studio, grateful for that slow graze of breeze just before the desert released summer's hasp to allow the sun its full reign. Rick with pale, untouched skin despite all the sun, a cell phone constantly at his ear (that distraction she used to refer to as his other lover), tending his grouping of citrus trees on the edge of their lot. The two of them eating breakfast with the windows open, hiking South Mountain on the weekends if Rick didn't have to work. Making love in the pool house after a late dinner, no distractions, no worries.

Slow. Unadventurous.

*　*　*

Unlike Jasmine, Rick has never been an attractive person. Especially in illness, the differences between them have become more pronounced. Jasmine walks into the study with a glass of water after his first round of chemotherapy and stands in the doorway while he throws up into the wastebasket at the foot of the sofa. She imagines what people must say about them now, now that he looks even older than before, his forty-nine to her thirty-six. His skin is pasty, waxen, the rings under his eyes dark, sunken crescents against his face. He lies back on the sofa in his suit pants and button-up shirt, adjusts the pillow underneath his head, then his body jerks and he sits up again, fast, and loses more of his stomach to the trash can.

"It's silly to think you'll get any work done," Jasmine says, and holds the glass to his face. She places the straw between his lips and he sucks the wetness through it.

Rick says, "It'll pass," and thanks her for the water. He says, "Think of it this way. Now I'll have an excuse for my receding hairline." He stands slowly and grabs the stack of folders from the desk, tells her he'll be home for supper.

Once Rick has left, their house is eerily quiet. Jasmine looks out of the picture windows in the study, overlooking the west bay of Oswego Lake, and imagines how quiet this house will be without Rick. No one—not Dr. Craftsman, not Rick, certainly not Jasmine—has used the word death, but it lingers in the foreground of everything they do, a moving, irksome presence they constantly brush away like an annoying insect, a presence that sooner or later will have to be acknowledged. Jasmine has never pictured this house full of children—any of the houses they've lived in, for that matter—but for some reason now, faced with the certain possibility of losing Rick to the pesky insect of death, she wishes there were other little bodies here.

She thinks about the three unfinished paintings in her studio upstairs, and opts for a run to Albertsons instead. Frozen waffles, skim milk, a bottle of Pepsi from the little glass-doored refrigerator next to the cash register. These are things she can handle.

* * *

The grocery store is empty except for a few well-dressed Lake Oswego moms, women with kids in the front of their grocery carts who speak to each other as they pass as if they are members of some secret club into which Jasmine was never initiated. Jasmine smiles gently at each one, looking, she knows, reserved and aloof. It's something she's never done well, making friends. In the two years that she and Rick have lived in Oregon, she's made very few. By the time she finds herself in the milk aisle, she realizes she needs to use the restroom, and the sensation is overwhelming—it's something that's happened since the cells in Rick's prostate started mutating and dividing rapidly, a sort of sympathy sense of urgency in her bladder. She asks an employee to direct her to the restroom, and he tells her to walk through the set of black swinging doors in the back of the store, past the employee break room, and through the small unmarked door just to the left of recycling bins that reek of alcohol and fermenting soda.

She undoes her belt buckle, sits, and relieves herself quickly, but not before noticing the white box sitting on top of the already full trash can. Against all reason, Jasmine reaches for it and sees that it is a box for a pregnancy test. She laughs at that, imagining one of the young checkers or even the teenage courtesy clerks being a panicked three days late, not able to wait until the end of her shift, crouching here in this dismal restroom and directing a stream of urine towards the end of the stick. Jasmine wonders if the girl even paid for the test. She drops the box back on top of the trash can and stands to wash her hands. But then she wonders, and can't believe what she does next. It's as if she's outside her own body, watching herself from some ethereal vantage: she sees herself pick the box up again and dig around inside with her fingers, and is surprised to find that the long plastic stick has been tucked back within the cardboard.

With her thumb and forefinger, Jasmine pulls the test from the box: a plus sign. The test is positive.

She has taken pregnancy tests before, twice. Both early on in their marriage, when she was several days late, and both times the test was negative. She'd peed on that little white tip and sat on the toilet, shaking, praying that there wasn't a little alien being taking shape inside her to alter her life as she'd built it. But this alternative she'd never imagined. She'd never thought about looking at the faint blue plus sign and feeling an opening up inside, a curious sensation akin to joy that settles somewhere within the small empty pockets of her body—the spaces between her collarbone and sternum, between the long, stringy ligaments in her hands, between her belly button and each bony hip. It's an overwhelming, rushing tide in which she envisions a tiny person coming from her own self while Rick's body shrinks inward and stops altogether, both at the same time. She opens her purse and drops the test inside before leaving the bathroom and reentering the world of the supermarket through the swinging black doors, an Elton John ballad on the overhead speakers, the overhead lights bright beyond reason. Jasmine squints her eyes, startled by the suddenness of it.

*　*　*

Within weeks, the chemotherapy has reduced Rick to a man who sleeps, lies on the sofa in his study, and pretends to eat for Jasmine's sake. For a few hours at a time, he tries to go in to work and morph seamlessly into the stockbroker he was a few months ago, but he comes home looking more ashen and defeated than when he left. Jasmine's sister, the only person from her family or Rick's that they speak with on a regular basis, calls to say that her three-year-old daughter has been telling people her uncle Rick has bees all over inside his body, and the doctors are trying to take them out. Her sister says, "Isn't that the sweetest thing? It's the only way her little mind can make sense of it."

That night, two flights above her sick husband in her little studio overlooking a small, man-made Oregon lake, Jasmine paints Rick: his top half is hot pink, and from the waist down she uses the brightest orange she can mix. She paints him nude, abstractly, arms and legs going in different directions, vigorous, thick, blue for his face, his sex a small, black line against robust orange skin. From his midsection fly bees by the score, faceless winged creatures with red on the tips of their wings. She puts her brushes down and washes her hands, embarrassed to have painted such a highly symbolic piece. It's something she would have painted in one of her college art classes—full of meaning, she would have thought, heavy-handed, contrived. She sits on her stool as motionlessly as she can, straining to hear sounds of Rick moving around downstairs. Anything will do: Rick shifting on the sofa, a cough, a laugh, heavy footsteps, the odious sounds of Rick vomiting. She just wants to hear him being.

As if on cue, Rick walks from the study to the kitchen, his footsteps slow but rhythmic, one after the other, the cadence of a thirsty dying man.

Outside the window, the rain makes its descent in soft, almost imperceptible drops, the bay and the houses on the other side shrouded in hues of gray. So dismally symbolic, she thinks, I couldn't paint a scene like this without laughing. She admits it to herself: she hates this place. The damp, the gray, the trees always so close, as if they are carrying out a secret sentry, privy to her every thought. She hears Rick walk back to his study and, she imagines, settle back into the burgundy leather of the sofa within.

Gently, trying her best to sound like the ever-caring wife, Jasmine calls down to him through the open door, "How you doing, sweetheart?" She hears him say something affirmative, his voice small and reedy. She pictures him smiling toward her studio, his cheekbones raised from malnutrition as if embossed on his face.

"Been painting?" he calls up.

"Little bit," she yells, then adds, "Nothing good." It's what she always says.

His answer, just as she expects: "It's always good." He pauses, and she thinks she can hear him shift his weight on the sofa. His next move, she knows, will be to wipe his forehead with his sleeve.

Jasmine leans back in her chair, far enough to grab the small bag leaning against the wall. It's where she's stashed the pregnancy test, along with a day-by-day pregnancy calendar she found on the Internet. Figuring the test taker was probably about a week late for her period, Jasmine had calculated that the baby would be born somewhere toward the end of September. She's marked the third week of September in her calendar with little stars as the expected time. Between now and then, each day on the calendar contains a little tidbit about pregnancy or childbirth, or sometimes marks a major milestone in the baby's development. By mid-February, the baby's elbows will form and its fingers will begin to develop; by mid-March, its hair and nails will start to grow, and its kidneys will produce urine for the first time. By the first of May, an ultrasound might be able to detect the baby's sex: three little lines between the legs were probably a little girl's labia; more obvious, a boy's penis would look pretty much as it would when the baby was born. Were it her baby, Jasmine would hope, she thinks, for a girl.

Rick would think she has lost her mind.

What started out as simple amusement, she realizes, has begun to take root as something more. It tentacles out and grabs her: were it her baby, she thinks, she'd suck on ginger lollipops to help with morning sickness. Were it her baby, she'd start buying things now from the children's boutique on A Street. Were it her baby, she'd name it Zoë, or Claire, or Brooke. Were it her baby, she'd hold it close, like this, against her breasts, and she wouldn't need Rick so damn much.

* * *

Jokingly, Jasmine's sister has always called her a kept woman. Jasmine can blame no one but herself for that. Still, she's never felt any guilt over it. After all, her first art professor freshman year had been adamant about the fact that all great artists were taken care of, spared the drone of daily, monotonous tasks (making money, paying bills, mowing lawns, nursing babies) by another human being. What woman could realistically devote her life to art if she was caught up in the minutia of every living second? So when Rick came along—older, established, endlessly kind and supportive—who could blame her for being swept up in it? Even now, Jasmine can't say it was love, exactly, at least not in a breathless and passionate shall-I-compare-thee-to-a-summer's-day kind of way. But he offered her a life when he asked for her hand, and she took it.

Jasmine never saw this as part of that offering. By the first of February, Rick spends twenty hours of each day in bed or on the sofa in the den. On the morning they are to go see Dr. Craftsman,

Jasmine makes scrambled eggs and toast, knowing full well that Rick will pick at them and drink the orange juice only. But she's trying. She's never had to take care of Rick before, in any way, and now the man can't even pull off his flannel drawstring pajamas without twenty minutes of deep breathing from overexertion.

Rick says, "Don't think I've ever seen you make breakfast."

"First time for everything," she answers. She offers Rick her hand, pulling him forward in the bed so he can sit up and eat. He takes a few bites, then dabs at the corners of his mouth with a tissue. Jasmine realizes she forgot to bring him a napkin. She takes the tray away and Rick pivots his legs over the side of the bed slowly.

"Don't, hon, I'll help you get dressed," she says as she heads for the closet.

"Jas, I can do it."

Jasmine pauses, uncertain how to read him. His face has gotten longer in the last month, the skin of his cheeks and chin hanging as if Rick were a seventy-year-old man, as if the bees inside him were spiraling downward, pulling his body in gravity's direction. Jasmine bends over and begins to tug at the hem of his flannel pajamas, but he stops her with a cold hand on her back.

"Jasmine," he says, "please. I'll meet you in the foyer."

She tries not to admit to herself that she's relieved he won't accept her help. From outside their bedroom, she can hear him rustle with his clothing for a minute, then stop, then rustle, then stop. By the time he comes through the door, she isn't sure how long it's been. She takes his hand and they walk together to the garage, where she watches him struggle with the door handle on the passenger-side door, struggle to pull the door closed, struggle with his seatbelt, but she doesn't offer to help him.

Jasmine doesn't like driving with Rick in the passenger seat; it's something she is wholly unaccustomed to. A rare break in the clouds has allowed the sun to shine down full force, and against the wet asphalt it creates a glare that is almost blinding. She drives with a hand in front of her eyes as they make their way up Bryant Road, and then the sun disappears and she relaxes into her seat a bit. She feels a warmth hit her back, and she sees that Rick must have turned on her seat warmer when he first got into the car. As they pass the Albertsons, Jasmine slows a little, watching a slightly overweight woman in her early twenties round up shopping carts from the wet parking lot. She looks hard at the woman's stomach, scanning for a slight bulge, even though she knows a pregnancy would rarely show this early, and then turns her attention back to the traffic. She can feel Rick looking at her from her right side, curious about her interest in the local grocery store employees. Without even looking back at the woman, Jasmine is convinced she isn't the one. She thinks she'd have a sense the minute she saw her, as if the very act of two women holding the same urine-soaked pregnancy test has bound them somehow, however inexplicably.

Dr. Craftsman is running behind by the time they reach his office. Jasmine and Rick sit in the waiting room with an older couple: a woman with short, spiky graying hair and a man who looks almost as sick as Rick. The man sits slouched with his feet outstretched, and the base of his neck leans awkwardly against the chair's back. His wife strokes his hair where it touches his forehead, looking at him while he sleeps. The skin on her hands is loose and pocked with brown spots. Jasmine is struck by the notion that she and Rick are unlike most other couples. She's seen so many of them since their move to Lake Oswego: couples who run together on Saturday mornings, garden side by side on Sunday afternoons. Pairs of people who start to look like a Picasso painting —their lines blurred, their limbs intertwined, as if they are really just one tangled entity.

"Rick Duchane?" the receptionist says his name with a question mark at the end, reading it from the top of a manila file folder. They stand without speaking and follow her to the doctor's office, where they take in his advice equally silently: advice that they stop the treatments and let hospice come into their home. Again, he doesn't use the word death. He doesn't use any phrases that even resemble death. The closest he comes is, "I think you should prepare yourselves." Rick won't move, won't meet her gaze. Jasmine thinks, Death is the beekeeper, and Rick is the outgrown hive.

*   *   *

When the hospice nurses start coming in shifts, Jasmine feels not only free to leave their sterile house on West Bay Road, but obligated. She feels as if she is in the way of all their contraptions, their pill bottles, the hospital bed they had brought in that Jasmine can't figure out how to operate when Rick needs his head up or his feet down. She finds herself walking the aisles of the Albertsons at different times every day, hoping to catch a glimpse of all the female employees on every possible shift. According to the calendar she downloaded off the Internet, this is the week the baby is about an inch long, and its heartbeat could possibly be heard by the doctor. She finds herself looking at things that are about that size: a large almond, a paper clip, a kumquat, a Tootsie Roll, thinking, The baby is that big already.

On a Wednesday morning, she leaves as soon as the nurse arrives, saying a quick good-bye to Rick and wrapping her black scarf twice around her neck. She drives into the Albertsons parking lot just as an employee (Jasmine recognizes her as the woman who works behind the bakery counter) leaves the store with her purse and coat. Something strikes Jasmine as she watches the woman make her way out of the parking lot and walk along the road, toward the small houses across from the gas station. She walks slowly, stopping every so often and looking down at the sidewalk. The rational part of Jasmine thinks this could be just a person hung over from the night before, but that part of Jasmine who can't stop thinking about the pregnancy test now tucked safely in the pocket of her coat knows that it's probably the inch-long fetus, busily forming organs, squirming its little limbs, the size of a perfect little Tootsie Roll, that is making her feel the way she obviously does. Jasmine keeps her distance, but pulls her car slowly out of the parking lot and eases into the gas station until she sees the woman turn into the driveway of a little bungalow with chain-link fencing and a mailbox painted to look like a cow.

Jasmine doesn't move for a long while after the woman goes inside. It's strange to her that after all this time, after all the imagining of the small being whose chemicals turned up the plus sign on that stick in her pocket, after wondering what it would be like for some woman to hold the child against a spit rag on her shoulder, to nuzzle its small lips against her nipples as it searched for food, she is one step closer to the actual thing. She thinks, So this is where the baby will live.

She can't think of what to do now. She can't go home, where even from her studio she would be able to hear the sounds of Rick and the hospice nurses shuffling here and there. They are the sounds of death, of the bees preparing for their final, momentous exodus from Rick's body. Rick would wonder why she had come home so soon, anyway.

She knows she should probably head to the art supply store and pick up a few more canvases. Her paintings have become so bright and the colors so gaudy of late that she's out of her sunflower yellow and brilliant orange, too. But she can't get herself to drive there. She heads the car toward Costco, thinking she can pick up a rotisserie chicken and some vegetables for dinner.

But as she turns off Seventy-second Avenue, she sees the bright Babies-R-Us sign and veers right into the parking lot instead. She hesitates for a moment as she drives past the front of the store, then boldly pulls into the frontmost parking spot marked with a sign: "Expectant Mothers Only." After all, does she not have the test in her pocket to prove it, should somebody challenge her?

The commercial world of childbearing is nothing like Jasmine would have imagined it. She is embarrassed when she thinks how she has never even been to a baby shower, aside from the one she attended in college when her roommate found herself unexpectedly expecting. Jasmine had put a ten-dollar bill into the pot, and someone else had purchased the roommate some large baby contraption (a stroller, or highchair, maybe; Jasmine doesn't recall). Since then, she's thought her solitary life as an artist was more than excuse enough for her lack of friendships, for the amount of knowledge she doesn't have about the rest of the world. Now, looking at row after row of rattles, diapers, shampoos, educational videotapes, and bouncy seats, she isn't so sure. Pregnant women and couples pushing babies in shopping carts idly stroll the aisles. The pregnant women walk with their hands on the side of their distending stomachs, rubbing ever so slightly as if the motion is mechanical, done without thought. Jasmine brings her hand to her own midsection, just above her waist, and lets it rest there.

Every day, she thinks, people are dying and having babies, and I am upstairs in my studio, splashing paint on a canvas.

She picks a stuffed brown dog from the bin of plush animals next to the cash register and uses her credit card to buy it. The cashier tucks the little dog into a plastic bag, bids Jasmine a good day, and moves on to her next customer.

Jasmine tries not to make any noise when she gets home with the plastic bag tucked under her arm, afraid of waking Rick if he's asleep. She creeps silently to the study, where the hospital bed sits in the middle of the room—between the leather sofa and the mahogany desk—and finds Rick awake but grimacing. The hospice nurse, an Indian woman in her midfifties, has the bed-sheets pulled back, and Rick's penis is lying across the side of the bed like a spent serpent, swollen and immobile. The nurse is eas-ing the catheter from within the diseased organ. When she finishes replacing the tubing, she pulls the sheet back over Rick's body (Rick, a man for whom modesty has always been primary) and runs a wet cloth over his forehead while he visibly relaxes into the pillows under his neck and back. Jasmine is frozen at the sight of this stranger's gentleness toward her husband. A feeling stirs in her, something akin to jealousy, maybe. Jasmine herself has never been that way with Rick. It never occurred to her to *want* to be that way with him, until the bees moved in, until dying, until now.

But the baby. A little bundled cluster of needs, entirely de-pendent on her. How easy it would be to give. How easily that gentleness must come. How easy to stroke that brow, small, new, pink. How easy to love so physically such a creature made up of little pieces of her own self.

* * *

In the way that he goes, Rick spares her. He dies in the same week the baby's sex is rapidly forming—though an ultrasound won't be able to detect it until months later, it is now, at the be-ginning of the eleventh week, Jasmine reads, that a tiny bit of tis-sue forms the external genitalia, which by the end of the week are recognizable, depending on sex. In fact, it's a big week for Jasmine in a lot of ways: the end of the first trimester, a major milestone, the end of morning sickness, if it ever reared its ugly head in the first place. And then Rick dies, quietly, overnight, no one else in the room.

Jasmine sits next to her husband when she finds him in the morning, his jaw hanging slack, his skin yellowed and waxy, in the middle of the study where he used to spend hours on the telephone or in front of the computer screen. She tries to recall the last thing he said to her, but it takes some time to think of the last conversation they had. Then she remembers: the previous morning, Jasmine had come into the study in her pajamas, before her shower, to say good morning before the nurse arrived. Rick had said, "Are those new pajamas?" When she shook her head, he looked at the ceiling and said, "You deserve new pajamas."

She deserves new pajamas. The last thing he said to her. Nothing pithy or sentimental, no quick recap of their fifteen years together. In fact, for the course of Rick's entire illness, they discussed the practical matters only, and never talked about the deeper things: the irony of the situation, the unfairness, the way it made either of them feel. And then it occurs to her that his actual last words, the last words he ever spoke, were likely not to her at all, but to the hospice nurse who had been here the day before.

She takes the hand towel next to the bed and dips it into his water cup, then with tremulous fingers runs the wet cloth over his brow the way she had seen the Indian nurse do a few weeks earlier. But his forehead doesn't feel like a forehead, and his eyes, open and frozen on the ceiling, disarm her. She knows, of course, that this wetness can be of no comfort to him now. Jasmine tosses the towel onto the desk and looks through the huge study windows, to the lake outside. The sky is bluer than she's ever seen it here, the water still. Three small birds swoop down from the magnolia tree to the left of the dock and fly low over the water.

Jasmine wants to see him, all of him. She moves the bedsheet slightly and looks at his body as if she's looking at a foreign object. Without life in it, it *does* seem like an object, like something she's never known. His arms, his hands, his fingers curled. His legs are stretched out, the toes pointed upward. She doesn't look further, under the flannel pajamas, at the line of hair down his chest, his enormously deep belly button, at the enlarged, ruined organ that started this business in the first place. But she does think about the last time she felt like she knew this body, the last time they made love, about six months before. He had been careful, attentive; she had hoped he would hurry it along so she could get in a few hours of work before bed. And then in the middle of the act itself, while he was wholly inside her and she was beginning to feel that familiar ache pulsing and building, Rick had yelled in pain and pulled out swiftly. He was diagnosed two weeks later.

She crosses Rick's hands on top of his chest and pulls the sheet up to his chin. So they're through with the business of dying, she thinks, and on to the business of death itself. A few weeks earlier, Rick had told her he had put together a Funeral Box. He said it that way, in capital letters, as if it was the last important thing he would do on this earth. And when Jasmine takes it out from under the desk, she sees that inside, he's put every detail together for his funeral. He's bought and paid for his casket months earlier (receipt included), written out a program for his funeral service (he wants it to take place in Phoenix, in the church where they were married), written his own obituary for the *Arizona Republic* and the *Oregonian* (he's included stamped, addressed envelopes for her to send these in). He has, in fact, left her with no details to worry about, no decisions to make, just as it has always been in their marriage.

How strange it seems to her that the box finally makes her cry, instead of the sight of Rick's body, hollow and spent as an abandoned hive.

* * *

Before she leaves for the funeral in Phoenix, Jasmine knows there's one more thing she needs to let die. She parts the dresses in her closet until she finds the plastic Babies-R-Us bag where she stashed it weeks earlier. The little plush dog, its nose flat like a pug and its fur silky soft, is still inside. Jasmine knows that here, in this house, this little toy will never have a baby's sweet face pressed to it, milky breath on its fur. She tucks the dog into her purse, its head sticking out, and checks to make sure the pregnancy test is still in the zippered coin pocket within. She finds it there, as expected, its blue plus sign growing paler and more indecipherable with each passing day. She knows it's probably a matter of weeks until the plus sign is gone altogether.

She backs the Volvo out into another gloomy, gray Oregon day, and drives to the small street next to the Albertsons, looking for the cow-shaped mailbox. She pulls the car to a stop in the driveway of the house, planning to leave the dog here quietly and be gone. In what she guesses must be the kitchen window, a woman's face appears and then quickly disappears. The house is a bright blue, almost turquoise, and looks like it hasn't been painted in the better part of a decade. Jasmine imagines a baby taking her first steps here, on the lawn next to her car, or there, on the asphalt driveway just next to the black-and-white-spotted mailbox. She is filled with a sense of rage, then, rage at the thought of *her* child being raised here, in this strange kitschy house.

By the time the woman has opened the front door, Jasmine has the Volvo in reverse. She drives quickly, away from the Albertsons, away from her empty house on West Bay Road. When she passes a park, she hits her brakes and pulls alongside the perfectly manicured curbside flower bed. The park is empty, but she imagines that on a nice summer day, the bright red plastic play structure, shaped like a pirate ship, must be crawling with squealing, delighted children. She imagines their mothers and fathers, standing to the side, shaking their heads, calling after them.

And then she's stepping out of the car, clutching her purse, staring at the empty sandbox, the empty picnic benches. And she thinks about Rick, about his hollowed-out body already on its way to Phoenix. She takes the stuffed dog and the pregnancy test out of her purse, and leaves them in the trash can next to the playground. She thinks: Now I am done.

*   *   *

Jasmine flies first class to Phoenix. It's what she's grown accustomed to, what Rick's investments and savings have assured her she'll continue to be accustomed to. The airplane lifts out of the Portland airport and makes a sharp lean to the right, giving her a view of the entire area, green-treed and majestic. From this vantage, she thinks, it's a spectacular place, far superior to the sprawl of rooftops and rock she knows she'll see as they touch down in Phoenix. Soon they are flying right next to Mt. Hood, so close Jasmine holds her breath for an irrational instant, wondering if they'll nick it with a wing.

That's when it hits her. She could go anywhere, now. She could stay here, in Oregon; she could go home to Phoenix. She could try somewhere new—New York, Chicago, another country. She has nothing to tie her to any particular place. She sees the decisions she can make—about everything from locale to long-distance calling plans—arc out in front of her: a new, different life, one she never imagined she'd want, replete with the fatigue of the mundane, the blessings of simple kindnesses, the ordinary need to wipe someone else's brow and mean it.

She drifts off to sleep, her neck bent awkwardly against the window. More than two hours later, while the plane passes over the Grand Canyon, she wakes startled, lunging forward with outstretched arms, grabbing at the air and the seat back in front of her. It takes her a second to realize where she is, and she curls her arms in against her body, embarrassed, wondering if anyone saw her jump. She's read about newborn babies doing the same thing. Fresh from its mother's body, a startled baby will flail its limbs outward and then clutch its hands desperately together: Hold me, it says. Of all the insatiable human urges, Jasmine thinks, is it any surprise that this one comes first? The urge to have another body wrap you in its arms, the fervent need to be held. The innate passion for flesh.

Jasmine puts a hand to her stomach, the way she'd seen the pregnant women do at the baby store. Soon, she'd be able to feel movement, were that pale blue plus sign in the park trash actually hers. The pregnancy calendar says it feels like tiny champagne bubbles floating upward, like popcorn kernels making soft, pillowy explosions.

Beneath her, the ground opens and closes in small fissures that jut off from the canyon, an awe-inspiring mass of red lines, like veins under skin. She presses her hand in a firmer grip against her stomach. A movement, quick, on her right side: she can feel it. Not bubbles, not popcorn. Wings. Lots of tiny little wings, in a mad frenzy of fluttering; or no, flinging outward, a desperate clutch for her attention. *I know, I know, there, there,* she wants to say with each kiss of wing, *soon, soon, we'll land.*

God and Birds

Police are investigating allegations of animal cruelty against a local teenager. A neighbor alleges the teen threw a clod of dirt at a duck, causing injuries that eventually required the duck to be euthanized.

—*Lake Oswego Review* police blotter

Sunday

MY FATHER MOVED out the day before I started high school, during one of the worst heat waves Lake Oswego had seen in years. My parents and I drove to church together in silence, while the heat rose from the road in front of us in small, translucent ribbons and then disappeared. My father let me and my mother out in front of the ward building and parked the car, meeting us again in the chapel, where my parents sat on either side of me, cold and unmoving as bookends. After the service, my father became animated again, all smiles and handshakes, whenever someone walked past our pew.

During Sunday school, I forgot about my parents altogether while I sat in the back of the room with Micah, our chair backs leaned against the wall and our shoes kicked off indifferently, fanning ourselves with folded paper. As always, the girls sat in the front of the classroom, among them Emily Wright, a girl whom I'd worked for years to impress with my disinterest. Micah was a master at making cracks at Sister Crawford while she taught, a woman in her late fifties who wore jumpers with animals embroidered on them and told us story after story about her kids. Micah would say things in a barely audible voice, out of the corner of his mouth, enough to fluster her but not enough to justify her getting him in trouble over it. I played along, snickering in all the right places, appropriately aloof. The last thing my social life needed was for the other kids to know that there was something I reacted to on Sundays inside that building, some unseen presence that I thought must be God, as if He were an invisible winged creature hovering in the corners, beating his wings gently and washing a calm over me that I felt nowhere else.

After we got home, I went straight for the kitchen and sat down with a bag of cookies and some orange juice. My mom disappeared to her room, and while I ate I watched my father pull two suitcases and a duffel bag from the front hall closet, already packed. He looked at me and said, "Your mom's a nut job," and left through the front door. As fourteen-year-olds go, I liked to think I was less naive than most; for years I'd been told I was smarter and more mature than my peers. I knew there was something lurking between them that would catch up to us sooner or later. But I'd always imagined the moment it happened: They'd pull me lovingly into the living room and we'd all sit on the couch together, like an awful after-school special. They'd say things like "Sometimes two people just stop getting along" and "This has nothing to do with you, Peter," and my mother would cry and they'd both hug me.

I didn't see my mom until around dinnertime, when we happened to pass each other in the hallway. Because of the heat, she was stripped down to the temple garments she always wore under her clothes, the hair around her face wet from sweat or tears, or both. She couldn't look me in the eye, but she offered to cook something, and I told her she didn't have to. She nodded as if to say thank you and ducked back into her room for the rest of the night.

The heat was sweltering. Even the breeze through the windows was torrid and angry instead of soothing when it hit my skin. Years later, as a journalism student in the Arizona desert, I would remember that heat wave as the worst of my life, the kind of gripping heat that gnaws at you from the outside in. I stripped out of my clothes, out of my briefs, and lay down on my bed face up, entirely naked, praying for relief.

Monday

My mom didn't come down for breakfast, and I waited as long as I could for her to poke her head out and wish me luck before I slung my backpack over my left shoulder, took an apple from the fruit basket on the counter, and rode my skateboard to Lakeridge in time for first period. By the time I got there, my shirt was wet with sweat where it hit my back, and the sun was already boring straight down as if it were high noon.

All in all, I didn't find high school too different from junior high, except the lockers were bigger and if you happened to walk through the senior commons at the wrong time, one of the big guys who high-fived each other and swore every third word made you do push-ups while they laughed. I figured that as a shorter-than-average, skinnier-than-average redhead, I was probably a prime target, so I made a point to avoid that side of the school altogether. There were some good surprises, though: Emily Wright sat behind me in Honors English, and I tested into fourth-year Spanish, a class with mostly seniors.

I ate lunch with Micah, who was ecstatic over three hot sophomore girls who had struck up a conversation with him during algebra. I was already beginning to sense the change that would take place in our friendship, since I had mostly advanced placement classes and would rarely see Micah during the school day. We waited in line and I got a packet of french fries, hot, and a Pepsi from the pop machine. I tried to join in while Micah pointed out every good-looking girl he noticed walk by the cafeteria, but in truth all I could think about was my mother. I wondered if she was awake yet, if she had gotten dressed, if she was ever going to be the same mom she had been. I wondered what she'd done to make my father leave in such an obvious fit of anger.

The bell rang, and I double-checked my schedule: fourth-period history. The two of us walked toward our lockers together, and out of the corner of my eye I saw a crisp twenty-dollar bill on the floor in front of me. Out of instinct, I bent to pick it up. It fluttered slightly just as it met my fingertips, and then seemed to race forward of its own volition. I stumbled over my own feet, leaning after it, and fell face forward onto the blue berber carpet. The commons around me erupted into peals of laughter—even Micah was bent over with it, his backpack falling off his shoulder as he shook. I looked up to see three senior boys, one of whom I recognized as

TJ Clark, our bishop's son. TJ wasn't laughing with the rest of them; instead, he had a sly smile on his face, a look like pride that he'd pulled off such a stunt.

Micah whispered, still laughing, "Dude, you got burned." He disappeared to the back of the crowd, not wanting to face with me the repercussions of my dive for the baited money.

TJ looked at me as if I were any freshman kid, not someone he'd known for over ten years' worth of Sundays and potlucks. He said, "Time for initiation, Freshman. Give me twenty." I shrugged my shoulders and started to walk away, sweat rolling from the tips of my red bangs and down onto my nose. Within seconds TJ had me pinned against a bank of lockers, demanding his push-ups, which I quickly gave him and then made my way to history. It was a small humiliation, and it was over quickly. Even so, it's a moment I returned to in college when a journalism professor had us studying the media hype that ensued after those two boys shot up their Colorado school.

The rest of the afternoon rode by in a haze of overheated classrooms and ringing bells that signaled our progression from class to class. Before I knew it, the final bell had rung. I pulled my skateboard from my locker and rode it home along Stafford Road, the air hitting my wet, clinging shirt like a welcome relief. When I reached the front door of my house—a vibrant, suburban red— there was a full minute before I turned my key in the lock when I forgot my dad wouldn't be coming in sometime after dinner, loosening his tie and settling in front of the evening news. When I really thought about it, it occurred to me that life without my father in the house wouldn't be too much different. Still, once I was inside, his absence was everywhere, turning up throughout the house like invisible viscous masses in the air that I had to hold my breath and walk through.

Tuesday

My mom was up before I was. When I walked out of the shower and blotted at my body with the old beach towel embroidered with my name, I smelled bacon cooking in the kitchen downstairs. The early breakfast surprised me; she'd been up late the night before, sitting with Bishop Clark and his wife in the living room. They spoke in hushed voices and smiled sympathetically whenever I happened to walk past on my way to the kitchen, and once, the bishop knocked on my bedroom door, saying my name softly, wanting to talk, but I pretended to be asleep.

The thought of my mom in the kitchen made me angry, as if she could wake up and pretend nothing unusual had happened in the house, pretend that I hadn't been an invisible casualty of whatever she'd done to drive my dad away. I wanted to make her wait, I wanted the plate of food she prepared me to become soggy and cold, solitary and uneaten on the table next to hers. I wrapped the towel around my waist and combed my hair down straight over my forehead, then swept it to the right and left it to dry. I applied deodorant, slowly, and tickled my ears with cotton swabs. The full-length mirror in front of me was still steamed from my shower; I ran a hand over it until there was enough clear space for me to see my whole body, and I unwrapped my towel.

I looked nothing like my father. Why hadn't I acquired in my genetic makeup his six-foot frame, his hair and eyes deep brown, like wet soil? My chest was still thin, hairless, and seemed to cave in upon itself. I turned sideways and looked at my upturned arm, fragile and stalwart as a dried noodle. My eyes moved down: my flat stomach, my hips, my small sex, topped with a sprinkling of red hair. By the time I dressed again, I was convinced by how little I resembled my dad that there must be some great family secret about my parentage that I was not yet privy to.

I went downstairs to find my mom smiling, waiting patiently, my cold plate of food on the table just where I'd imagined it would be. She was sitting a few feet off the ground, on a stack of granite tiles my dad had brought in weeks ago with the promise to re-place her kitchen counters for her.

She said, "Sorry I've been such a mess, Pete." I shrugged my shoulders. "Do you want to talk about it?"

I was silent for a minute as I dug into a piece of bacon, then said, "Where is he?" My question seemed to take her aback; she expected something deeper, something about the whys and hows of our family breakup.

"He's in a little apartment. End of McVey, on the lake." She looked down at her hands, then up at me. "How was school? You like it okay?" I shrugged again and finished my last bite of egg, then stood and made my way to the front door. She called after me, offering me a ride, but I told her I preferred going myself. I'd come to realize the past few days that my mom was treating me the way most adults tended to, as if I were much older despite my tiny stature. I suddenly wished I could dumb down my speech, take the regular classes with the rest of the kids, anything to get her to offer me the attention a child deserves when his parents are at odds. I stepped onto the front porch and felt for the first time since I had woken up that the air had lost its fiery sting. Gray clouds hung above my head and I almost wished I'd grabbed a jacket.

I wasn't surprised about his apartment. My father had told me once he always wanted to live on the lake. He'd taken me way out just over the crest of Bull Mountain, where the houses be-come farther apart and the marshlands begin. Dusk began to settle as we sat on the hood of the brand new Honda his company had given him. And as the sun worked its way closer and closer to the horizon, the air around us was suddenly filled with ducks, so many that it was hard to see the sky between them as they quacked and made their way back to the slough that stretched before us. It was a sweeping, majestic site, one that filled me with an awe I hadn't known before. I thought about how small and insignificant we were on the hood of that car, while around us the world went about its natural business, every day. Every now and then one of the ducks would fly lower than the others and we could see the patterns on its underbelly. The peace I felt was similar to the calm that washed over me and made my legs tingle on Sundays when the bishop or my teachers talked about God and Jesus, about the way everything on the earth was in accordance to their grand scheme, their carefully executed plan.

My dad must have felt it, too, because he said to me, his eyes still on the thousands of wings above us, "You stay close to the Church, son, you'll be all right." And then, on the drive home, he told me he'd always tried to convince my mom to buy a home on the lake because he'd love to watch the birds come and go, but she couldn't get past the hazards of water. Sitting there, on the black leather seats of my dad's Accord, I slumped my shoulders and tried to make myself invisible against the night sky, ashamed because I was like her. All I could see when I thought about a life on the water were those hazards: drowning, floods, toxic runoff. A life on the edge of something utterly beyond my control.

Wednesday

It turned out my father did call, in the morning before I left for school, to ask how I was and ask me if I wanted to spend the weekend with him at his new place. I left for school feeling almost normal again, having heard his voice, feeling hope for the first time that things might work out after all, and he'd come home. I let my mom drive me to the high school after I hung up the phone, feeling the threat of rain in the clouds that hovered above the house.

Sure enough, the rain started to fall by third period, when I walked across the street with the rest of the Mormon kids to the ward building for seminary. The older girls linked arms and ran in front, their jackets pulled up over their heads, while Micah and I dawdled as far behind as we could. Micah tossed a Hacky Sack back and forth between his hands and said in a hushed voice, "People must really think we're freaks." I shrugged my shoulders and pretended I didn't care either way, but I did wonder what the rest of the student body at Lakeridge thought of the grand third-period exodus of Mormons. The only thing that gave me comfort was knowing some of the more popular kids, TJ Clark included, were walking among our ranks, so we couldn't be considered all that strange.

Our seminary teacher was a man in his midtwenties from a neighboring ward, dressed in a suit and tie as if we were here for Sunday services, not just in the middle of the week for religion classes. He outlined the year for us: we'd be studying the New Testament, starting with the four gospels, as a way to get to know Jesus better and learn to live like He did. I got all warm inside when he said that, the way I always did when I thought hard about religion and the unseen mysteries of life. During the last five minutes of class, Bishop Clark came by to wish us all a good school year and tell us we were doing the right thing by being there. He stepped aside and watched proudly as TJ gave the closing prayer, his arms folded and his head bowed as if he had nothing to feel sorry for in the world. The bishop shook everybody's hand as we filed out of the seminary room to head back across the street, and he gave me a tight squeeze on the shoulder that told me he was thinking about what was going on in my family. It was an unwelcome reminder.

By the time I got outside, Micah had already run across the street to escape the rain that was beating down even harder than it had been an hour before. I stepped into the road slowly, not caring about the water as it cascaded down the sides of my face and pounded a cadence into the pavement around me. I felt a hand on my shoulder and turned quickly, expecting Bishop Clark again. Instead I saw Emily Wright, who seemed as unimpressed with the cloudburst as I was.

"How are you?" she asked, and I wondered what she had heard about my parents, if she was feeling sorry for me.

"Good," I answered, sounding too cheery, and immediately I regretted it. I hoped she didn't think I was being sarcastic. "You?"

"Yeah, okay," she said. She tucked a wet strand of hair behind her ear as we reached the other curb. She was pretty even with her hair wet and stringy along her face, but it was more that had always drawn me to her. She was this strange anomaly, a stereotypical Mormon girl to the core who was number seven in a family of ten and answered every question in Sunday school and always wore a CTR ring on her left hand to remind her to "choose the right." At the same time, though, I'd overheard her recite full sets of Eminem lyrics and work words like damn into her conversation as seamlessly as anybody. I was about to ask her if she was headed to lunch when I felt a soft blow from behind and landed on my knees in the wet pavement. I heard TJ's voice behind me and turned to see him swinging his backpack in the air in front of him, saying, "Stay on your toes, Freshman."

Emily rolled her eyes and was nice enough to look away while I got to my feet and brushed off my backpack, sending water flying in all directions. She told me she'd see me in English and joined a group of her friends as they headed to the cafeteria. TJ ran off as quickly as he'd come and I was left to my own devices, feeling humiliated not because I was a target, but because he'd succeeded in the most uninventive, ridiculous ways.

Thursday

If God were a great winged creature, the kind I had imagined Him to be, I was beginning to doubt the span of those wings, the infinite comfort available in those downy feathers.

I left for school early, refusing my mother's offer for a ride despite the fact that the rain had continued to fall at an even pace since the morning before. It was too wet to skate, so I walked. But instead of turning right at McVey Road, I took a left, knowing I could get to the apartments where my dad was staying as quickly as I could Lakeridge in the opposite direction. I knew he wouldn't be there; I couldn't remember the last time my dad was still home past six in the morning, even on a Saturday, but I wanted to see his place. I wanted to see this place I had imagined him in the last four days. I'd pictured him downcast and spiritless, wandering aimlessly on a back deck that looked out over Oswego Lake, thinking about me and my mother. I'd pictured him waking up early to a quiet, empty room, returning late at night with no one to watch him work at the knot in his tie. Though he had left our perfect little Sunny Hill home, somehow I couldn't help feeling that it was my mother and I who had abandoned *him*.

Before I reached the end of McVey, I could feel the wetness down to my socks, and I enjoyed knowing that to the passing cars, my drenched hair looked more brown than red. Every so often I'd wipe the water from my eyes where the drops clung to my lashes and then run my hands over the thin nap of corduroy on my pants, which didn't do much to dry them off because my pants were so wet themselves. The Bay Roc Apartments were at the end of McVey, just before the park. I knew because my mother had pointed them out for me the night before, after she picked me up from the weekly youth activity at the church. I didn't know which unit was his, but I figured I'd sit in the parking lot for a while and come up with my next plan, which I knew didn't involve going anywhere near school.

I passed the Lake Oswego Corporation Building, where the boats that bore the city's logo sat docked and ready to work, weather permitting. I looked out at the lake, following it inland until I saw the back end of Bay Roc, where the units overlooked the water. I rounded the front of the complex. And then I saw something that surprised me: my dad's Accord parked out in front. I wiped the wetness from the face of my watch: seven forty-five. The fact that he was at home could only mean he was worse off than I'd imagined.

I read the unit number from his parking space and knocked on the corresponding door. When a woman opened the door wearing a towel on her head, I thought I'd made a mistake, but after a moment of silence the woman must have realized who I was because she said my name. It caught me off guard, that this beautiful woman, petite and red-cheeked, would know me, and then I heard my father's voice from somewhere in the apartment behind her.

I froze. For the third time this week, I was the lead character in a bad after-school special, only I hadn't rehearsed the part.

Should I have stayed? All I could think to do was turn and walk away slowly. I don't know if my dad saw me, and the woman didn't make a move to stop me. I didn't want to face him, to hear the lines I could have written for him: "I was planning to tell you this weekend," or even the old standby, "This isn't what it looks like." Even before my interest in journalism, I knew all about a good cliché.

Years before, when he took me to witness the majesty of the ducks returning to the marsh at dusk, I was filled with a sense that God had ordered the universe in ways I would never understand, that I was a part of mysteries beyond my very imagining. Standing in the parking lot of my father's new home, I felt smaller than I ever had, a naive, lost child, dripping wet with rain. The only common thread that bound the two events was the consummate knowledge that what I understood about the world I could hold in one hand, loosely, and it was liable to slip through my fingers at any moment.

From my vantage, the surface of the lake was hazy and rippled wherever the rain touched it, forming tiny lines like the nap of my corduroy pants.

Friday

Micah convinced me to go to the Stake Dance, which was an easy task mostly because I was afraid if I stayed home, my mom would corner me into a conversation. I didn't think my dad had told her what had happened the day before, because she hadn't made any mention of it, and I wanted it kept that way. I knew I should have felt sorry for her, sided with her, even, but learning about my dad's indiscretions only made her a greater target for my anger.

Micah's mom dropped us off at the church. As we approached the doors, I could already feel the bass beat from the music inside. The adults at the door had us show them our dance cards, and the group of girls who came in just after us were asked to kneel on the ground to assure that their skirts could touch the backs of their calves.

I danced with Emily Wright twice—the first time because she asked me, and the second because her friends pushed us together for the last song. Her hands were warm and clammy and she acted as if it were the most natural thing in the world, us dancing together after knowing each other for years but hardly speaking at all. She rested her head on my shoulder during a long instrumental solo and asked me if it was true, what she'd heard about my dad.

"You mean that he moved out?" I asked.

A moment of silence between us and then, "Did he mess around on your mom?"

So it was a pity dance. I felt a sinking somewhere in my body, like something vital had turned to stone, but the clammy grip of her fingers held me tight and I accepted her kindness, however short lived. I wanted to pull her closer. I thought about the fireside we had months before, when the stake president had given us a PowerPoint presentation about preserving our morality. He'd drawn a red line, a line we were not to cross.

Keep your hands to yourself, he'd said.

Kiss your girlfriend the way you'd kiss your mother, he'd said.

The feelings you have are normal, but aren't to be acted on except between two married people, he'd said.

Emily tossed her hair slightly so it brushed my shoulder, and I felt the stirring of an erection that left me virtually paralyzed with fear. I tried not to think about what went on inside my father's lakeside apartment, about what exactly he did with the towel-haired woman, the one younger and thinner than my mother.

Saturday

My mom wouldn't let me get out of visiting my dad. When I pressed her for a reason, her eyes welled up and she said, "Because

he's your father and he loves you, that's why." We reached a com-
promise: I'd go as long as I could take Micah with me. I knew his
presence would ensure that my dad couldn't bring up my visit the
day before last.

The weather had taken another turn, and where it had begun
to feel like autumn it was now all sun and heat again, as if we had
been given one last taste of our summer vacation. It was probably
the weather as much as a desire to avoid my father that made me
break my end of the deal. Micah and I left the house with the full
intention of skating to the Bay Roc apartments, but ended up
rounding the bend and following State Street until we reached the
fountain at Millennium Park. There were grade school kids in
swimsuits running through the fountain, shrieking each time the
water crept higher than they anticipated or another child splashed
them. Babies held onto their mothers' fingers and toddled through
the smaller streams of water. We held our skateboards in our arms,
having been lectured before by a patrolling officer that skating
wasn't permitted in the park.

Micah said, "Wish we'd brought some soap."

We laughed. "That was awesome," I said, and we nodded in
agreement. Early in the summer, we had loaded a Tupperware
bowl full of dish soap in Micah's backpack, and I hung back on
the steps to the lake while Micah nonchalantly poured the soap
into one of the grates of the fountain. Within minutes, the fountain was a mass of foaming bubbles, like a volcano spuming froth
and lather, instead of the quaint arcs of clear water it had been
moments before.

We took to the steps of the lake again, this time only to hang
out and kill some time. I put my board on the step above me and
kicked off my shoes in order to sit with my feet dangling in the
mossy water. In front of us was a sign, etched in brass: *Private
Lake, Please Stay on Steps*. While Micah leaned back and looked at

the sky through his sunglasses, I thought how strange it was that such a large body of water could be considered entirely privately owned. How the people in this town owned Oswego Lake piece by piece, depending on where their property lines were, which easements they held. I thought about what our seminary teacher had made us read out loud about Jesus and the Sermon on the Mount, about the earth being the Lord's footstool and the thing the meek would inherit.

Did the fact that my father now lived with a deck over the water give me partial ownership? Could I dive in from these steps and claim I had every right now to this private lake? Apparently my father's leaving us gave me entrance into a club I'd only viewed from the outside in.

A flock of ducks floated leisurely towards us. Just a foot in front of my feet, a school of tiny silver fish spun in what looked like choreographed circles. I swung my feet out at them, making their small bodies scatter outward, then sunk my feet deeper until they touched the submerged step below them, rubbing my bare soles against the slimy moss that clung to the cement.

"Check this out," I said. "This is disgusting." Micah plunged his feet down and grimaced with appropriate repulsion. He submerged his hands next and started pulling the moss from the step in long strings and tossing it at me, so I stood and ran off the steps to the landscaped dirt mounds to the left of us. The ducks swam in circles and squawked, obviously annoyed by our commotion. Two of them lifted their wings as if ready to take flight and beat their feathers against the water.

"Hey, duckie, duckie," Micah called, picking up a small rock and hurling it toward the water. "Have some bread."

"How dumb do you think they are?" I said. The biggest duck plunged its emerald green head into the water and stayed that way for a full five seconds, its back end sticking straight out of the lake.

Micah said, "Check out Mr. Duck Ass over there," and I laughed.

We sat still for a minute and the ducks came toward us again, this time looking at us as if expecting a meal. They must have been tossed tidbits from this vantage on a daily basis. I picked up a hard piece of dirt from the mound and held it in my hand. It was warm from the sun.

I'd like to say I was thinking of my father with another woman in his bed, the bishop's son holding my hands behind my back and shoving me against a locker bank, when I pitched the solid clod toward the group of birds floating in our direction. But in truth, I was thinking only about the strength of my arm, about how far I could likely fling the thing, about how much I wanted to be accurate, about the shock that would register on one of those duck's faces when it was spread with a shower of dirt.

"Holy crap," Darren said as the big green-headed duck made a noise I'd never heard from a duck before and took to the air. The rest of the birds scattered, some jumping in the air for a few feet and landing again, some swimming off fast toward the center of the lake. For a second I doubted whether I'd even hit the big duck at all, but then I watched it slow its flight and drop to the water just feet in front of us. Behind me, a woman I recognized as someone who lived down the street from me ran down the steps and used my skateboard to pull the duck toward her from the water. Her daughter stood behind her, watching, no older than five.

I wondered how much the woman had seen.

I felt a coldness start in my back, between my shoulder blades, and radiate outward. I couldn't get the picture of the duck out of my mind—unconscious, its feathers raised, the underside of its wings a vivid, radiant purple. That night, I would dream of him:

all greens and purples, feathers unsettled, his expression pained as he plummeted back toward the water. Later would come lectures from my mother and even from Bishop Clark about respecting living things, about how serious a thing I'd committed. But in the moments after I held that warm clod in my palm and brought the alpha duck down, I felt a certain elation I haven't felt since, except in remembering. As I stared at the limp bird, my seminary teacher's voice ran like a track in the back of my mind: The earth is the Lord's footstool. And then I turned the voice off, and Micah and I ran.

The Weight of Bones

Vandals put a dead bird in a mailbox on the
5800 block of Stewart Glenn Court.

—*Lake Oswego Review* police blotter

THE SKULL STARES down at Ellen from the exposed ceiling of her charred garage, its eye sockets smooth, hollow voids. Ellen blinks, then squints her eyes, unsure if she is seeing what she thinks she is. It takes only a few seconds for her to gather courage to climb the ladder rungs and ease the thing out from between the scorched wooden beams. She dusts the gray, ashy residue from its yellowed surface with her fingers, and then holds it in both hands, a solid, heavy thing. Would a human skull be this heavy? Ellen knows nothing of the weight of bones. For all she knows, a human skull, free from its charge over the brain and its marrow long since dried, could be light as honeycomb. But it *looks* human, and that is enough to convince her. In fact, despite its lack of life and flesh, Ellen has to turn her face away, because the skull looks as if at any instant it could wink at her, or inexplicably break into song.

Should she feel alarmed? The only alarm she feels is in rela-
tion to how normal it feels to be standing in her destroyed garage,
holding what must be a human skull. It's the same feeling she had
earlier in the week, when she rounded the corner of her street and
realized the fire trucks were parked in front of *her* house, and not
one of her neighbors'. Seeing the orange flames pirouetting from
the top of her detached garage felt like witnessing any other daily
suburban event. For all the panic she felt, she might as well have
been thinking: Oh, look, the cat has left a mole on the front
porch, or Good, the landscapers are here—see how nicely they've
trimmed the laurel hedge.

Ellen rubs her fingers along the back of the skull where three
tiny cracks meander through the bone. She looks to the rear of
the garage. Through the hole in the wooden frame the firefighters
created with their axes, Ellen can see Oswego Lake: green, mo-
tionless, unsuspecting.

*   *   *

Because her daughter is home from college on spring break, Ellen
has to be careful about the skull. She carries it into the house
under her arm, hidden by the bulk of her cardigan, then takes it
upstairs to her bedroom and places it gently in the bottom drawer
of the bureau, where her husband used to keep his sweat pants
and running shorts. She knows the right thing to do would be to
call the Lake Oswego Police Department and hand the skull over
to them. It would, she knows, be the story of the century in this
upscale suburban town, where the police officers are more skilled
at disposing of sick raccoons and giving parking tickets than investigating possible homicides. But if the last year has taught Ellen
anything, it is that the old rules no longer apply. This is a world
where your husband of twenty years could up and leave you for a

young, blond art teacher, where the garage of the home your grandfather built eighty years ago could burst into a sudden panoply of flame, where human remains could appear in the charred ashes and virtually drop into your palms, like a gift.

Ellen changes her clothes and makes her way to the kitchen to fix dinner. She finds Heather there, sitting at the kitchen table, flipping through a magazine: Heather, who in the right light looks the same to Ellen at nineteen as she did when she was three and just out of diapers. Heather closes the magazine and leans back in her chair, tossing a quick glance at her mother, and then rolls up her sleeve to pick at the dry patch of eczema on her right elbow—an old habit. Ellen has noticed that Heather has become rather adept at looking as bored as possible since she came home. From the other side of the kitchen, Ellen hears her ex-husband's parakeet scratch at the bottom of its cage and then squawk. Apparently Dean's new lover has a hysterical phobia about birds, so Ellen is stuck with the thing, and she can't seem to gather the courage to get rid of it.

Heather pulls her sleeve down over her elbow again and walks over to Lily's cage, sticking her fingers through the skinny bars. "What's for dinner?" she asks.

Ellen replies, "Aren't you going to your dad's tonight?"

"Stop it, Mom." Heather opens the door to Lily's cage and lets the bird walk onto her hand. Lily turns her orange neck and stares at Ellen with her speckled black eyes.

Ellen musters the most neutral voice she can. "Hon, you've got to see him at least once."

From Heather, who looks like a pirate with Lily now perched on her shoulder: "Stop it."

There are times when Ellen thinks Heather might feel even more betrayed than she does herself, as if Heather had been the one, not Ellen, who walked in on Dean while he had another woman straddling his lap, naked except for a thick winter scarf and long, dangling earrings. She counts this as a blessing: were their child younger, she thinks, they would have to fight for Heather's affection, shield her from the messy truth of divorce. But Heather is old enough to understand what her father has done, and while Ellen is careful to play the part of selfless mother and encourage her daughter to maintain a relationship with her father, she secretly loves Heather's anger. It's nice to have an ally in the house, if only on Heather's brief breaks from school.

Even so, in a deep part of herself, Ellen is worried about a possible shift in Heather's loyalties. Ellen started stocking the pantry with all of Heather's favorite foods in the weeks before she came home from school, almost unconsciously giving her a reason to stay in the house instead of spending time with Dean. Take tonight, for instance: even knowing Dean had invited Heather to dinner, Ellen has planned all day on making enchiladas and Spanish rice, Heather's favorite meal since she was in grade school. There are two gallons of chocolate milk and a six-pack of Mountain Dew in the fridge, Oreos and Nutter Butters in the cupboard above the stove. Last night, Ellen let Heather drink half a glass of wine with her fettuccine alfredo (favorite dish number two).

"Enchiladas! Score," Heather says when she notices Ellen pulling the corn tortillas from the refrigerator and opening the cans of red and green sauce. Heather puts Lily back and settles once again into her magazine at the table while Ellen dips each tortilla in sauce, fills it with cheese, and rolls it into a casserole dish. Lily lets out a series of small, melodic chirps.

Ellen can feel the skull, like a third presence in the house. For a brief moment, the house feels like it did a year and a half ago: the dusk settling in the air around them, like a comfortable old blanket; Ellen chopping and sautéing the evening meal; Heather pouting at the table; Dean sitting upstairs in front of the television or computer, the third family member they couldn't see or hear but could always count on.

Except tonight, Dean is not Dean. Dean is a human skull with its bottom jawbone missing and three hairline cracks along the cranium, just under what was once a head of hair.

Dean as a skull. Dean utterly exposed, reduced to nothing but his inflexible inner skeleton. No fleshy, dimply grin. No flesh at all.

Ellen smiles to think of it.

*   *   *

The discovery of apparent human remains in her garage is complicated by the fact that the house has been owned and occupied by Ellen's family, and Ellen's family alone, since it was built in the late twenties. Her Grandpa and Grandma Mosley, who were among the first year-round residents of Lake Oswego, built the home on the shores of the lake, and both died young, leaving it to Ellen's parents. When Ellen's parents retired to a condominium community in Arizona five years ago, Ellen, Dean, and Heather moved into the house. Strangely, Ellen feels a certain thrill when she thinks that if this heavy chunk of human bone is the result of some sordid homicidal event, it's likely that one of her family members was at the heart of it.

Ellen has the skull on the desk in the study when she hears a knock at the door. She's been turning it over and over in her hands for the better part of an hour, comparing its shape and form with pictures of human skeletal systems on the Internet. She's hoping to decipher how old the thing is, what happened to it, if it could really be something else entirely. The knock startles her, though, and she jumps forward in her seat, inadvertently pushing the skull off the desk. It lands on the old fir floor with a sturdy thud that seems to echo across the study, and then begins to roll slowly toward the wall, in the direction of the floor's slope. It comes to a stop on the edge of the rug, pieces of the rug's fringe resting in its left eye socket. It takes only a second for Ellen to lunge from her chair and scoop it up in her hands, inspecting all of its yellowed parts for signs of damage. By now the doorbell is ringing, her visitor clearly impatient. She hides the skull under the desk and closes the door of the study behind her.

It's Dean on the front porch. Ellen silently curses herself for not imagining this possibility and checking for any sign of him before she answered. But here he is, and they find themselves face to face for the first time in over a month; for the first time, actually, since Dean stuffed his clothing and tennis rackets into various bags and suitcases and left his house key behind.

He lifts his chin and tries to look past her. "Is she here?"

Ellen squints her eyes and raises her shoulders: a question.

"Heather, Ellen. Is Heather here?"

Ellen is quiet, and then, "She's out for the day. Boyfriend's up from Eugene."

"She didn't come for dinner last night."

"She didn't want to."

They stand in the doorway together, the silence long and awkward. Dean looks the same, which surprises her. He is still Dean: the same man who hung this front door himself three years ago, who rebuilt this front porch with his own hands. He pushes his bangs back from his face with a quick sweep of the hand, a habit he's had since they met in college twenty years ago. She notices he isn't wearing his wedding band.

He says, "Tell her I came by, okay?" and turns to leave without waiting for a response. This is what really gets to Ellen, what has fueled her anger more than anything in the last months: Dean's complete lack of penitence. Shouldn't a cheating husband, once caught, act at least remotely sheepish, be racked with guilt? Shouldn't he feel sorry, if not for falling in love with someone else, then at least for getting caught straddled by a woman who writhed like a whore? Shouldn't he even ask about his damn bird? Ellen closes the door and watches him through the window as he walks to his car. His gait is swift. She notices him gesturing with his hands in front of his face, as if talking to himself.

Which is when she sees what she should have seen the minute she opened the front door: there, in the front seat of Dean's old Land Rover: the art teacher, hopelessly blond, patiently waiting with her window rolled down. As beautiful with her clothes on as she was with them off.

Ellen sees them both as they were. Flesh everywhere. Breathing desperately, moving to a rhythm she could no longer hear or feel.

Ellen sees them stripped of all that flesh, reduced to nothing but their thick, rounded skulls, solid and earthbound as stone.

* * *

Ellen knows little of her grandparents, except that her Grandpa Mosley owned the first market, tavern, and men's clothing store in Lake Oswego. And that he was a drunk, at least according to her mother. Is this a recipe for homicide? It's hard for Ellen to say. In pictures, he wears a brimmed hat pulled low and doesn't smile, looks as if he has an edge to him, the kind of man who could potentially knock somebody off without too much residual guilt. Then, of course, there are her own parents, but the worst thing

Ellen can imagine them doing is teaming up with other residents to get someone kicked off the school board. Could they have covered up somebody else's crime? Ellen has a few uncles she can picture getting into trouble, and in some ways she can envision her parents disposing of the evidence—more for the sake of their own reputation than from any sense of familial loyalty.

Somehow, though, it's a mystery she isn't bent on solving. Just knowing that somewhere in her family line could be a haggard, violent moment, shrouded by years of secrets, is enough to make the hair at the nape of her neck tingle, enough to send a thrill through her own heavy bones. She's more curious about the victim than she is about the criminal. She's slowly building an identity for the skull: most of the time it feels female, young, afraid. But whoever it was, Ellen can't bring herself to feel pity; after all, there's a sort of strength and perseverance in this, in turning up years later in the rafters of a stranger's garage.

After Dean has come and gone, Ellen finds herself in the burned-out garage again, a place the fire officials have warned her it isn't safe to be. But she needs to know: what else of this person might be in here? She moves the ladder carefully to the place where she first spotted the skull and climbs it slowly. Why hadn't she thought of it sooner? Her fingers shake as she combs through the insulation and blackened wood, but she finds nothing. She looks at the opposite side of the garage, the side where Dean used to park his Land Rover. There, the roof is gone entirely, and where there were once rafters and shingles is only a large hole through to the sky. Whole bones could have been lost in that fire, she thinks. She moves the ladder to the hole and slowly raises the extension, leaning it gently against an intact beam. She climbs straight through and finds herself looking over the top of the garage, out toward the lake. A light rain is just starting to fall, and the little drops create pinprick disturbances on the water, making the surface of the lake appear mottled and wavy. She turns her face upward and lets the rain coat her face. She closes her eyes.

When she opens them again, it's because she hears a car door close. Looking over the garage, she sees Heather and James, her boyfriend of five months, standing in the driveway and staring up at her.

Heather looks embarrassed. "Mom, what the hell?" she says, and Ellen climbs down the ladder, back through the roof of the garage, back to the smooth cement floor. When she comes out the side door, Heather and James have already gone inside, so she follows along the covered brick path to the main house. In the kitchen, Heather has taken off her sweater and left it lying on the table, and James is rubbing her back with both of his hands in slow, deliberate movements.

Ellen asks, "You two sticking around for dinner?"

Heather doesn't make eye contact with her mother. "I think we're going to Dad's."

Ellen is silent for a minute and then says, "What changed your mind?"

Heather takes James's fingers into her hands and rubs them. "James did," she says. "He keeps trying to convince me it's unhealthy not to at least confront Dad and let him explain." After a long pause, as if explaining herself, Heather adds, "Did I tell you James is a psych major?"

Ellen smiles and looks from Heather to James. "He's absolutely right," she says. "I've been trying to get her over there myself."

James excuses himself to use the bathroom and Ellen sits in the chair across from Heather's. Behind her daughter's head, she can see a squirrel stealing seeds from the bird feeder she hung in the garden window, its thick tail twitching in rhythmic waves against the rain. Heather clears her throat. "He's right, I think, Mom," she says, and Ellen nods.

"What else does James tell you?"

"James says you're probably stashing all this anger up inside in a hidden place and it will come out sooner or later."

"Does he?"

"Yeah. He says it's healthier to let it out slowly, as it comes."

Ellen imagines the anger coming out of herself slowly, the way air leaks from an almost-sealed balloon in a hissing stream, deliberate and steady. She is startled out of the strange image when Lily apparently notices the squirrel outside the window and lets loose a sequence of earsplitting squawks.

She's still squawking, her orange feathers ruffled upward, when Heather and James leave through the mudroom. James has his hand on the bare skin at the small of Heather's back, just under her shirt. Ellen feels a sinking inside herself, on the left side just under her heart, to see him so comfortable with her daughter's flesh.

* * *

The fourteen bones at the front of the human skull hold the eyes in place and form a person's facial features. This is one of the facts about the human head that Ellen has learned from the Internet. She is fascinated by the way every human skull has facial bones that come in pairs, one on either side of the nose, the reason for symmetry in the human face. She feels the bones in her own face: just above her brow; at the top of her jaw; the hard ridge where eye socket meets cheek. She's always been happy with her face, always known she was an attractive woman by the looks she still gets from random people in the grocery store, the jealous comments of other women. She runs her fingers over the facial bones of the skull in her lap and tries to envision the flesh that covered them —how dainty was its nose? How even were the apples of its cheeks?

Dean's new lover could likely piece together the mystery. Just over a year ago, when Ellen still thought she had the perfect, healthiest marriage, Dean enrolled in a sculpting class at Marylhurst because it was something he'd always wanted to do but had never had the chance. He'd come home after the first class raving about how good his instructor was, how amazing she was with the human form. For months, as they drove to church or home from the grocery store, Dean would point out this woman's art where it sat in public parks or in front of city buildings. He was thrilled when she'd asked Dean to stay after class and be a model for a piece she'd been commissioned to sculpt for Westlake Park. "You should see her work," Dean had told Ellen one night when he came home. "She'll spend like an hour just on a single eye." He was amazed at how lifelike she could make something look with just her fingers and a few slabs of wet clay.

And now, fourteen months later, Ellen is amazed at the change in her life.

She doesn't worry about whether Dean's clothes have been washed and pressed.

She doesn't spend her weekdays focused on which shade of red would look best in the study, or making phone calls for upcoming homeowner association meetings.

Instead, Ellen has been having—what can she call them?— murderous thoughts. She has always heard that divorce does strange things to people. But this? She thinks about Dean in the bathtub with a plugged-in hair dryer, his lifeless arm draped over the porcelain side. She thinks about Dean in the cockpit of an airplane headed in a perfect nosedive into the side of a cold, remote mountain. She sees him drinking a cup of coffee at the Starbucks on State Street, only later to find it was laced with arsenic: his limbs go cold and numb, his lips twitch.

Ellen goes so far as to wonder what she can pull off. Would they find a body weighted down at the bottom of the lake? Could she stage a spectacular accident over the guardrail of a rural highway, Dean and his art teacher plummeting over the side?

She sleeps with the skull in the slide-out drawer under her bed, an empowering, warming presence below her.

* * *

Ellen hears Heather and James come in late, past midnight. Were they at Dean's the whole time? She hears them talking low and laughing, and then she hears footsteps upstairs to Heather's bedroom, the heavy sound of a door closing, then nothing. The mom she was a year ago would have cared that her nineteen-year-old daughter was spending the night with her boyfriend in this house. Ellen used to think about propriety, about right and wrong, about the importance of principles and reputation.

She turns over in her bed and closes her eyes, hoping to seduce sleep into letting her in. Beneath her, the skull burns into the underside of her bed.

Heather and James are probably tangled in the sort of embrace she'd never wanted to imagine her daughter being part of. It feels like a slap in the face—that her daughter would do that here, in her house, after the series of sordid events that have reduced her marriage to crumbs, good only for sweeping away. Suddenly she finds herself wanting to eat, wanting to comfort herself with something from the refrigerator or pantry. She climbs out of bed and pulls a bathrobe over her pajamas.

The kitchen is cold; she's grown accustomed to heating only the upstairs of the house at night. Ellen digs around in the refrigerator until she finds the pan of leftover enchiladas, then scoops some onto a plate, covers them with plastic wrap, and pops them into the microwave. While she waits for the microwave to beep its finish, Ellen rinses the dishes that are piled in the sink and loads them, one by one, into the dishwasher. Just as the beep sounds, she sees it: Lily, lying on the bottom of her cage, unmoving. It seems odd to see the bird this way. Ellen hasn't ever paid the thing much attention, but she's pretty sure she's never seen it sleeping on the floor of its cage.

As she moves closer, Lily's wide, unblinking eyes and slightly spread orange wings give her away: the bird is dead. And her first thought goes to Dean. For the slightest of moments, Ellen feels bad for Dean, knowing that this will be anything but welcome news. It's a gut reaction that angers her.

Ellen opens the door of the cage and pulls Lily from the paper towels on the cage floor. She's got white bird poop on her left side, where she was lying on the towels, and the rest of her feathers are stiff and glossy, untouched. She could almost be a stuffed bird, a flawless little monument on someone's mantel, every feather in its place, but for that messy left side.

What to do with the bird? She could call Dean, but he's probably sound asleep with the tiny little art teacher perfectly spooned into the front of his body. The image sends a reflex of nausea through her body.

Ellen is methodical in her exploration of the bird. She gets out the heart-shaped cutting board, the one she reserves for meats and fish, and the sharp butcher knife from the wooden knife block on the end of the counter. It takes longer than she would have thought to get Lily's head off—not one clean slice, as she was anticipating. She finds herself having to saw the thing back and forth through the flesh under the feathers, and then pound the bird a bit against the cutting board to get through the bone. She isn't fazed by the mess of orange tufts and red blood on the board and her hands.

She needs to get the skin and feathers off. She pulls her five-cup glass measuring pitcher from its perch in the cupboard above the stove, fills it with water, drops Lily's head in, and puts the whole thing in the microwave. She has to remove the enchiladas first (a surprise to her: she'd forgotten). It takes a good seven minutes before she sees it at a full boil, Lily's head hopping around in the bubbles like a meaningless piece of debris, like an old fishing bob in the surf. She pulls the measuring cup from the microwave and uses a slotted spoon to remove the head, leaving it on a paper towel next to the sink to cool. She is pleased to see that most of the head feathers have come off in the boiling water, and imagines how easy it will be to remove the skin from Lily's skull.

The death of Dean's bird, she thinks, how utterly Godfather-ish. If only she'd thought of it herself, instead of finding the thing dead of its own accord.

*　*　*

Lily's skull, once Ellen cleans it of its outer baggage, is so light it barely registers when she holds it in the cup of her palm. It's smaller than she would have imagined, roughly the size of a seed-less grape or a chocolate-covered macadamia nut. If she bends her fingers in and grips hard enough, Ellen knows, she could crush it with one hand, cracking the bones like a nut to reveal the tiny bird brain inside. And yet Ellen is struck by its form, more so than with the human skull. She likes the streamlined way the skull comes to a point at the front, where Lily's beak would have been. The bones come together to form what looks like an arrow, like something with somewhere to go, something with mysterious destinations.

Ellen wraps Lily's headless body in an old plastic grocery sack and keeps the skull in the palm of her hand as she makes her way outside through the mud room. The rain has stopped, but the air is moist and heavy with its absence. Ellen stands in front of what used to be her garage door—now a messy, blackened mound in the driveway. She closes her eyes and sees the flames as they vaulted skyward from the garage roof and the thick billows of gray smoke as they filled the air. How easily such an old, established structure burned.

She climbs into her car and heads south, where the road follows the shoreline of the lake and then veers away from the water altogether. She drives through Lake Grove, seeing through her windshield the neighborhoods she's known since she was a child, until eventually she slows as she passes the house she knows Dean and his new woman are renting together. She's seen the house in the dark before; in the first weeks after Dean left, Ellen would drive this street with her headlights off and watch for signs of life inside. The most she ever caught was a brief silhouette behind the curtains, a cat clawing at the front door. Once she thought she saw Dean dragging garbage cans to the curb, but she floored the gas pedal and left before she could verify it was actually him.

She leaves her headlights on tonight as she pulls up alongside the mailbox. Here, she thinks, Dear Dean, is my gift to you. She unfolds her fingers and places the delicate bony structure inside the metal box and then closes the lid. But something makes her hesitate. She'd planned to throw the rest of Lily's body in the trash, but why give Dean the good stuff? She removes the skull, careful to keep it intact, and instead leaves what's left of Lily's orange headless body, which he can have. A skull is a mystery, a permanent thing, and she wants that for herself.

CPSIA information can be obtained at www.ICGtesting.com
Printed in the USA
LVOW11s0406240215

428083LV00005B/289/P

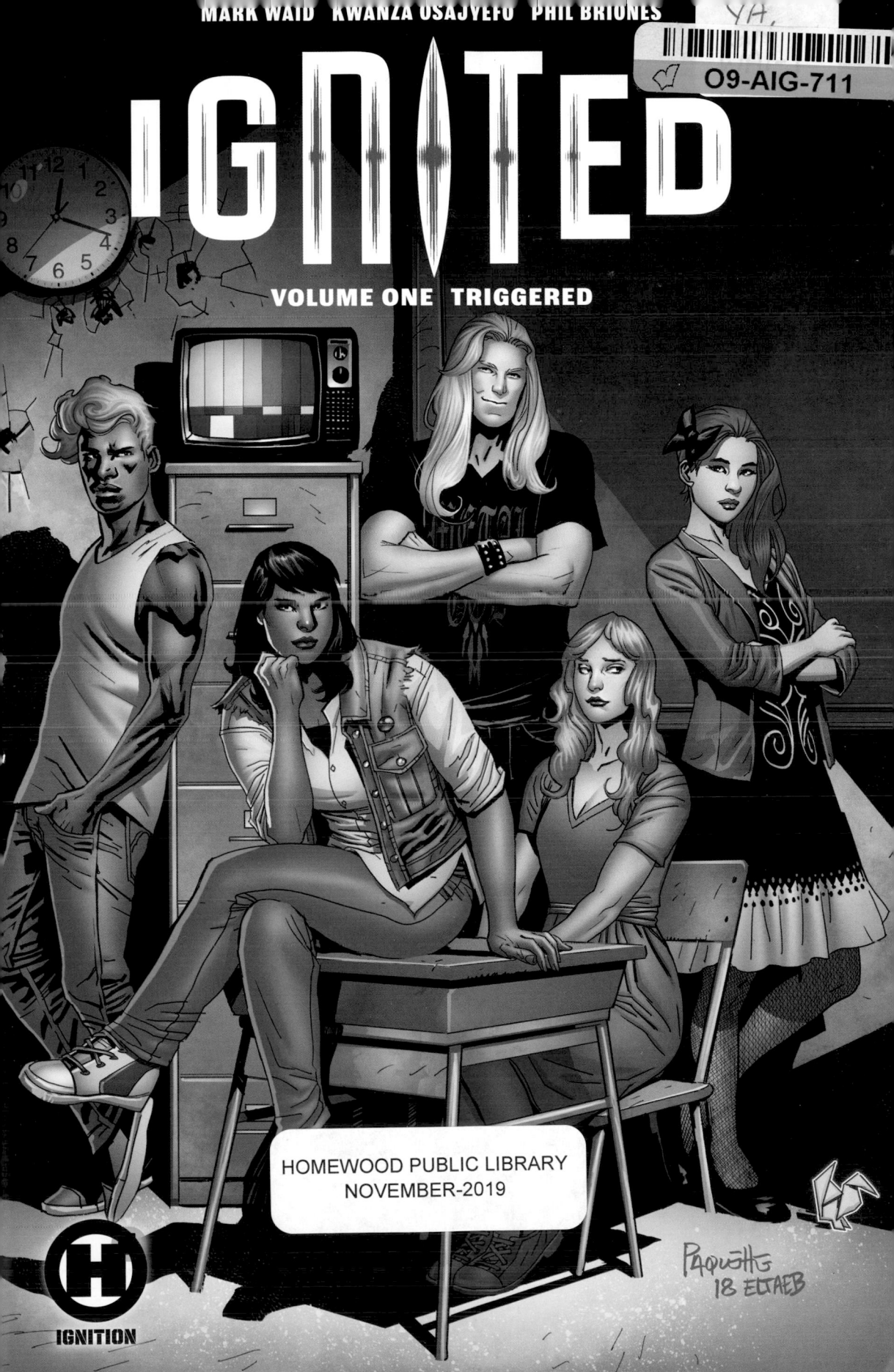

IGNITED

WRITERS | **MARK WAID** AND
KWANZA OSAJYEFO
ARTIST | **PHIL BRIONES**
COLOR ARTIST | **ANDREW CROSSLEY**
COVER AND PAGES 2-3 ILLUSTRATION |
JOHN CASSADAY AND **PAUL MOUNTS**
LETTERS | **A LARGER WORLD STUDIOS**
TITLE PAGE AND PAGE 4 ILLUSTRATIONS |
YANICK PAQUETTE WITH **GABRIEL ELTAEB**
AND **LEONARDO PACIAROTTI**

SHARED UNIVERSE BASED ON CONCEPTS CREATED WITH
KWANZA OSAJYEFO, CARLA SPEED MCNEIL, YANICK PAQUETTE

DIRECTOR OF CREATIVE DEVELOPMENT | **MARK WAID**
CHIEF CREATIVE OFFICER | **JOHN CASSADAY**
SENIOR EDITOR | **FABRICE SAPOLSKY**
ASSISTANT EDITOR | **AMANDA LUCIDO**
LOGO DESIGN | **RIAN HUGHES**
SENIOR ART DIRECTOR | **JERRY FRISSEN**

CEO AND PUBLISHER | **FABRICE GIGER**
COO | **ALEX DONOGHUE**
CFO | **GUILLAUME NOUGARET**
SENIOR ART DIRECTOR | **JERRY FRISSEN**
DIRECTOR OF SALES AND MARKETING | **AILEN LUJO**
SALES AND MARKETING ASSISTANT | **ANDREA TORRES**
SALES REPRESENTATIVE | **HARLEY SALBACKA**
PRODUCTION COORDINATOR | **ALISA TRAGER**
DIRECTOR, LICENSING | **EDMOND LEE**
CTO | **BRUNO BARBERI**
RIGHTS AND LICENSING | **LICENSING@HUMANOIDS.COM**
PRESS AND SOCIAL MEDIA | **PR@HUMANOIDS.COM**

IGNITED VOL 1: TRIGGERED This title is a publication of Humanoids, Inc. 8033 Sunset Blvd. #628, Los Angeles, CA 90046. Copyright © 2019 Humanoids, Inc., Los Angeles (USA). All rights reserved. Humanoids and its logos are ® and © 2019 Humanoids, Inc. Library of Congress Control Number: 2019909800

This volume collects IGNITED issues 1-4.

H1 is an imprint of Humanoids, Inc.

HUMANOIDS

THIS IS NORMAL.

PROPERTY OF ANOUK LOVARI

THIS IS NORMAL.

THIS IS NORMAL.

MILK

THIS IS NORMAL.

IT'S IMPORTANT YOU KIDS FEEL SECURE.

EVERYONE'S NERVOUS. EVERYONE'S TWITCHING. JUMPING AT EVERY NOISE.

THAT'S WHY EVERY ROOM HAS BEEN EQUIPPED WITH AN *EMERGENCY KIT* TO KEEP YOU *PROTECTED.*

LET'S SEE WHAT'S *INSIDE.*

STRUGGLING TO STAY CALM.

WHAT'S GOING ON WITH OUR PLANET?
- NATURAL DISASTER MAGNIFYING
- MAGNETIC FIELD FLUCTUATING
- THE SLEEPING SICKNESS OF HOUSTON - TX.

THERE'S... A SMALL WOODEN WEDGE FOR THE DOOR.

THERE'S ALSO A *HAMMER.*

AND SOME *DUCT TAPE.*

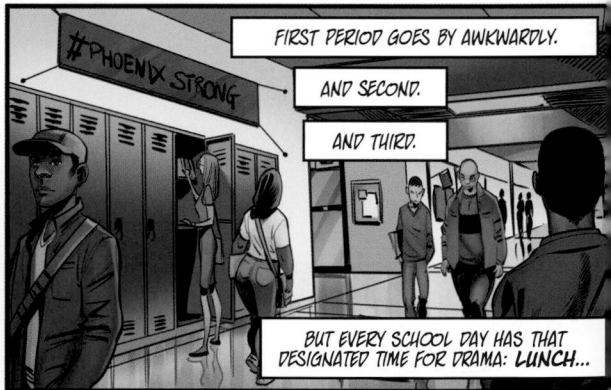

FIRST PERIOD GOES BY AWKWARDLY.

AND SECOND.

AND THIRD.

#PHOENIX STRONG

BUT EVERY SCHOOL DAY HAS THAT DESIGNATED TIME FOR DRAMA: *LUNCH...*

AND THAT'S WHEN THE *JACK-IN-THE-BOX* BURSTS OPEN.

PING PING PING PING PING PING PING

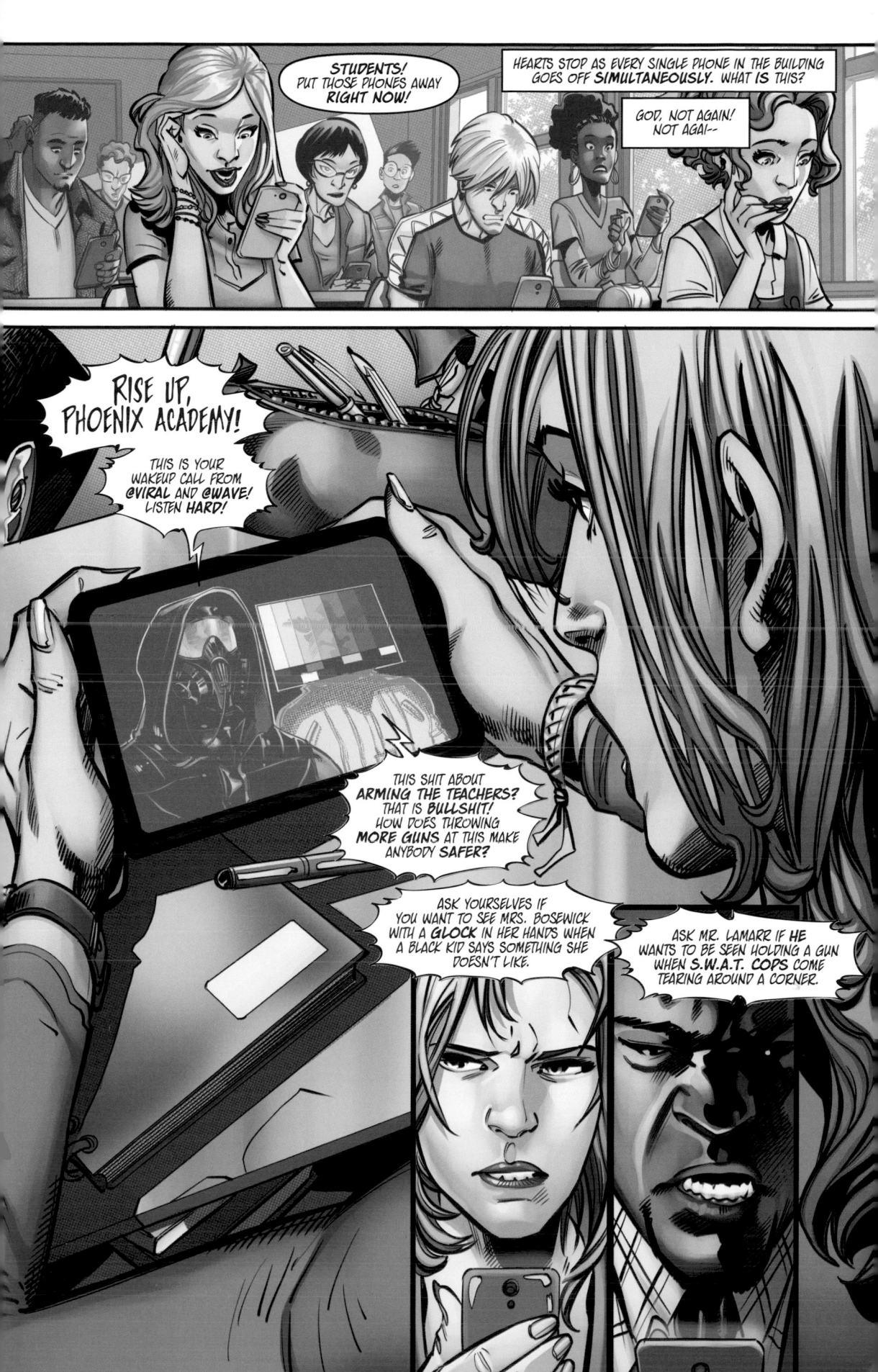

LOVELY WORK, HIMARI.

ANOUK, HOW'S YOUR PROJECT COMING?

ANOUK?

HMMM?

BRRRINGGGGG

OH! I'M SORRY! I--I--

MISS LOVARI, ART DOESN'T MAKE *ITSELF*.

I WANT YOUR MIND *AND* YOUR BODY IN MY CLASS ON MONDAY. UNDERSTOOD?

YOU ARE *OBSESSED* WITH VIRAL AND WAVE. WHY?

IS THAT STRANGE?

? DID YOU JUST... DID YOU JUST ASK ME A *QUESTION*?

THAT'S *ELEVEN WORDS*. THAT'S TEN MORE THAN ANYBODY CAN REMEMBER YOU SAYING ALL LAST *YEAR*, LITTLE QUIET ONE. WHY SO *CHATTY* ALL OF A SUDDEN?

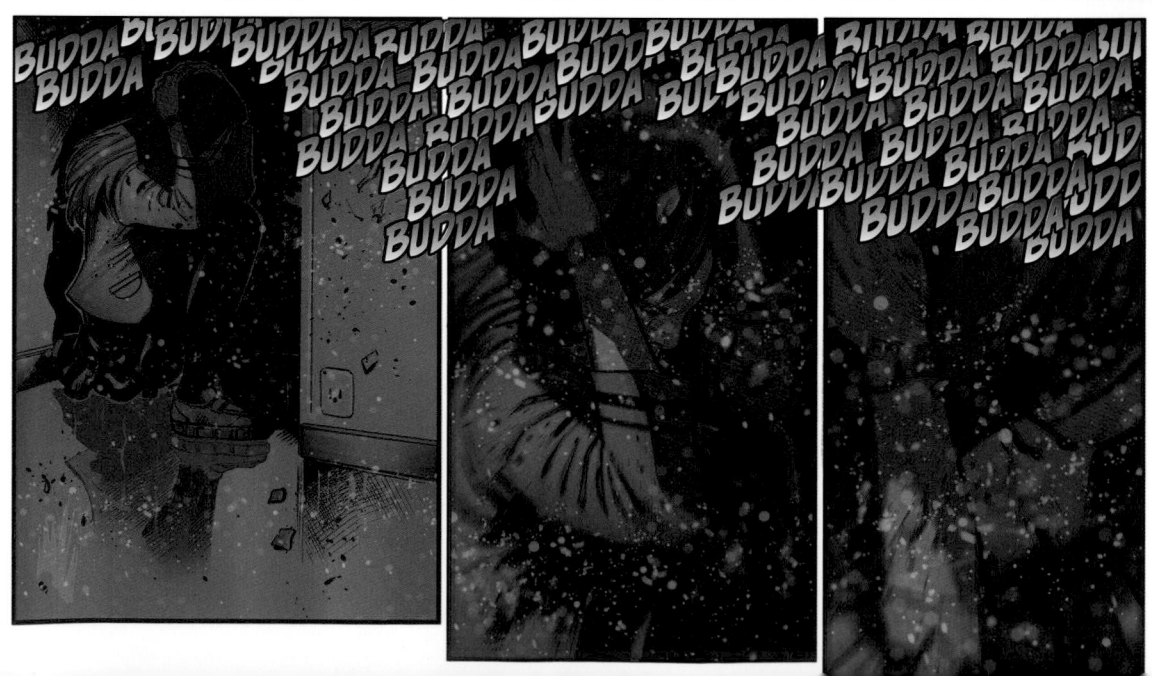

BUDDA BUDDA BUDDABUDDA BUDDA BUDDA BUDDA BUDDABUDD BUDDA BUDDABUDDA BUDDA BUDDA BUDDA BUDDABUDDA BUDDA BUDDA BUDDA BUDDA BUDDABUDDA BUDDA BUDDA BUDDA BUDDA

JAR.

SWEAR JAR.

I'LL OWE. DAD, WHAT ARE YOU *DOING?*

WHAT THE SCHOOL BOARD *WON'T.*

WE'VE *DECIDED.* IF THEY'RE NOT GONNA KEEP OUR KIDS SAFE, THEN *WE WILL.*

DAMN STRAIGHT. NO CRAZY-ASS SICKO'S GONNA GET WITHIN A *HUNDRED YARDS* OF MY *MELINDA,* OR FELIX'S *SAMMY,* OR ANY OF YOU KIDS.

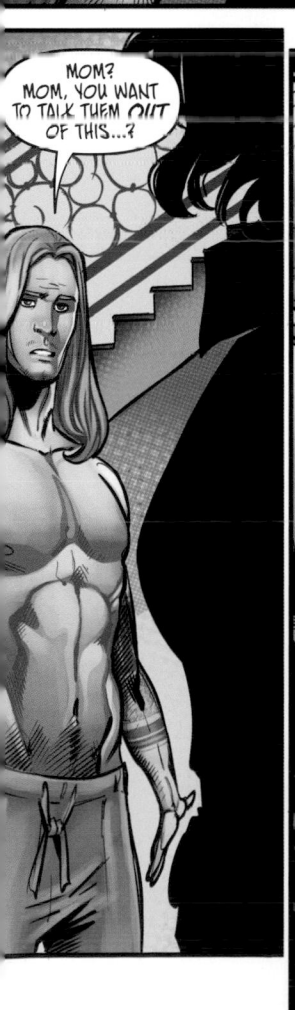

MOM? MOM, YOU WANT TO TALK THEM *OUT* OF THIS...?

NOPE.

FAR AS I'M CONCERNED, THESE MEN ARE OFFICIALLY DEPUTIZED AGENTS OF THE *COUNTY.* MY *COUNTY.*

ANY OTHER SMART-ASS QUESTIONS?

LUTHER, *HUSTLE.* WE'RE LEAVING IN *FIVE.*

I'LL *WALK!*

2

THIS YOURS?

NOT TALKING? IT'S YOUR RIGHT.

IF ILLEGALS *HAD* RIGHTS.

THE SHIT YOU'RE IN...

YOU'LL WISH DEPORTATION WAS ALL YOU HAD TO WORRY ABOUT, CHICA.

¡OYE PENDEJO!

CAN THEY SEND SOMEBODY 'SIDES YOUR *JUAN VALDEZ* ASS TO PANDER TO ME?

YOU THINK YOU FUNNY, BITCH?

TENEMOS UN VIDEO DE TI EN ESTA MÁSCARA DE LUCHADOR, EXPLOTANDO COSAS*.

YOU'RE GONNA BE CHARGED WITH SOME DOMESTIC TERROR SHIT.

WHUMP

*WE GOT VIDEO OF YOU IN THIS LUCHADOR MASK, BLOWING SHIT UP.

HaHAha! SOY MENOR DE EDAD**, PUTO.

**I'M A MINOR, BITCH.

¿PERO TIENES VIDEOS...NO?

¿LOS VISTE, CONO?***

***BUT YOU GOT VIDEOS... RIGHT? DID YOU WATCH THEM ASSHOLE?

SHIT.

Been helping CALLUM in the meantime

until I figure out WTF is wrong with me

MATE. YOU...

...YOU NEVER SAID ABOUT THE *PARENTS* THING...

THIS IS *MESSED UP.* THIS ISN'T *HAPPENING.* THIS--

AND WHAT ABOUT *YOU?* DID YOU MAKE THE TEACHERS *SICK?* HOW--

ATTENTION ALL STUDENTS! ORDER HAS BEEN RESTORED!

RETURN TO YOUR HOMEROOMS NOW! REPEAT-- RETURN TO YOUR HOMEROOM!

I-- I HAVE TO GO--

HEY--

I HAVE TO GO, OKAY? I--

I WON'T SAY ANYTHING. JUST ONE THING, THOUGH.

HE SAID HE SAW WEIRD LIGHTS. YOU, TOO?

YEAH. WHY?

ANOUK?

GOD ALMIGHTY. THAT ONE KID'S TURNED INTO A **WALKING CELL TOWER**. I DON'T EVEN **KNOW** WHAT **CALLUM'S** STORY IS.

WHAT DO THEY THINK THEY'RE **DOING?**

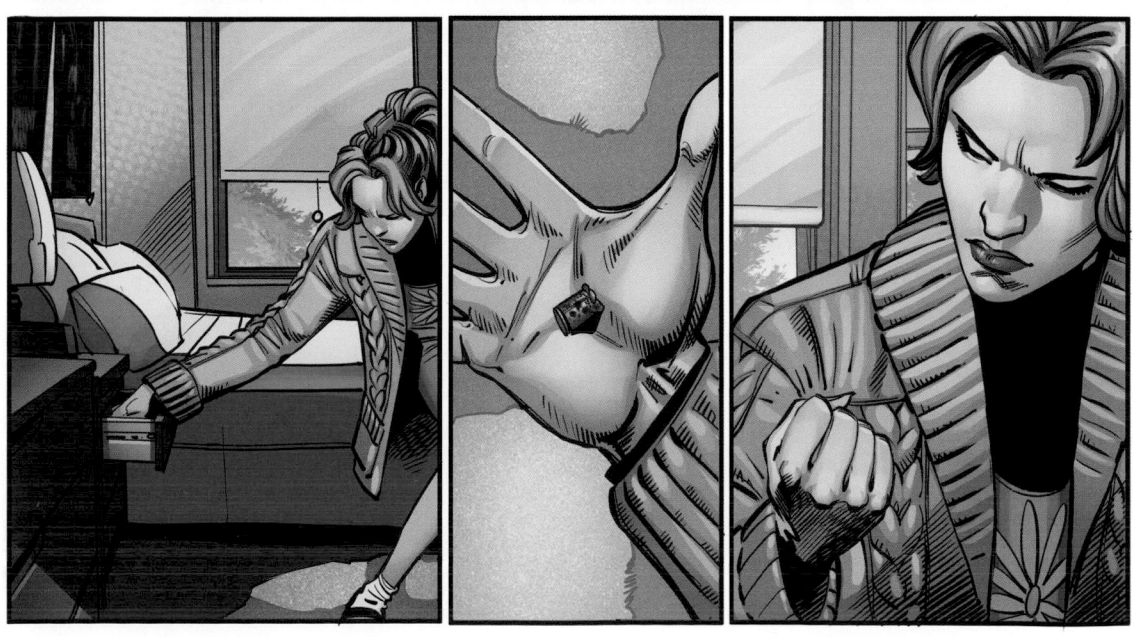

THIS ISN'T NORMAL.

OH, COME ON.

COME ONNNNNN...

THANK YOU.

BRIIIIING

NOW, WHERE SHOULD I--

HEY, GIRL.

LONG *TIME* SINCE I'VE SEEN THAT SWEET *GRASS* OF YOURS.

OH, *GROSS*. THIS GUY. DALE. DAVE. SOMETHING.

DAD HIRED HIM TO DO SOME *YARD WORK* OVER THE SUMMER UNTIL I CAUGHT HIM PEEPING THROUGH A *WINDOW*.

I'M GOING TO THROW UP.

WANNA TAKE A LITTLE "STUDY BREAK" WITH ME TONIGHT?

WOW, IS THAT COLOGNE OR PAINT THINNER?

FECK OFF, WANKER.

GKKK

YOU MOTHERFUCKER.

C'MON. ASSHOLE NEEDS TO FOCUS ON A LITTLE CHLAMYDIA KICK-UP 'STEAD OF BITCHIN' ON YOU.

THAT'S YOUR IDEA OF KEEPING A LOW PROFILE?

WHEN HAVE I EVER BEEN "LOW PROFILE."

YOU, THOUGH...

I TOLD YOU, I WOULDN'T SAY A WORD. I WAS LOOKING FOR YOU TO... TALK MORE ABOUT THINGS. BUT YOU HAVE TO TELL ME--

--YOU'RE LIKE SHAI TOO, RIGHT? HOW'D YOU GET THIS WAY? WHAT DID THE LIGHT DO TO YOU? I...I NEED TO KNOW.

...

FECK. ALL RIGHT.

NOT KILLER. A SCATTER WARNING.

BETTER THAN **TEAR GAS**, I GUESS. WHAT DO YOU THINK?

WHOA! WHERE ARE **YOU** GOING?

THAT WEIRD LIGHT AROUND WHATEVER HE'S **DRIVIN'**? INNT THE SAME WEIRD LIGHT THAT CHANGED YOU 'N' ME?

MAYBE **TANKBOY** THERE KNOWS WHAT'S GOIN' ON WITH US.

WAIT.

I'M COMING **WITH.**

TEEF. YOU'RE...

YOU GOT A POWER **TOO,** THEN?

NOPE.

BIG HELP AGAINST **BIRDS** THEN.

STAY BACK, YE DAFT--WE DUNNO THIS GUY'S--

DUDE!

UNEXPECTED.

YEAH! BIG FAN, DUDE!

HKKKK!

FINALLY, WE *MEET! BROTHERS* IN THE *CAUSE!*

NO OFFENSE, GIRL I DON'T RECOGNIZE.

NONE TAKEN.

VWOOP VWOOP VWOOP VWOOP

MAN, DO I HAVE QUESTIONS!

I JUST HAVE *ONE!*

FZAAAK

YAAAH!

KZAAAK

ZZZKk

AAAH!

AAAAH.

OH, MY GOD.

CHOOM CHOOM CHOO!

MY PRAYER JUST GOT ANSWERED BY A *SENTIENT ELECTRICAL* SIGNAL.

IT'S SHAI.

CHZKKKT

CHZKKKT

YOU HURT?

WHAT THE HELL--?

HELL, YEAH, I'M HURT! EVERY-BODY TAKE COVER!

EVERYONE'S WATCHING THE SUDDEN FIREWORKS. WHICH MEANS--

--NO ONE'S LOOKIN' AT US! RUN!

RUN!

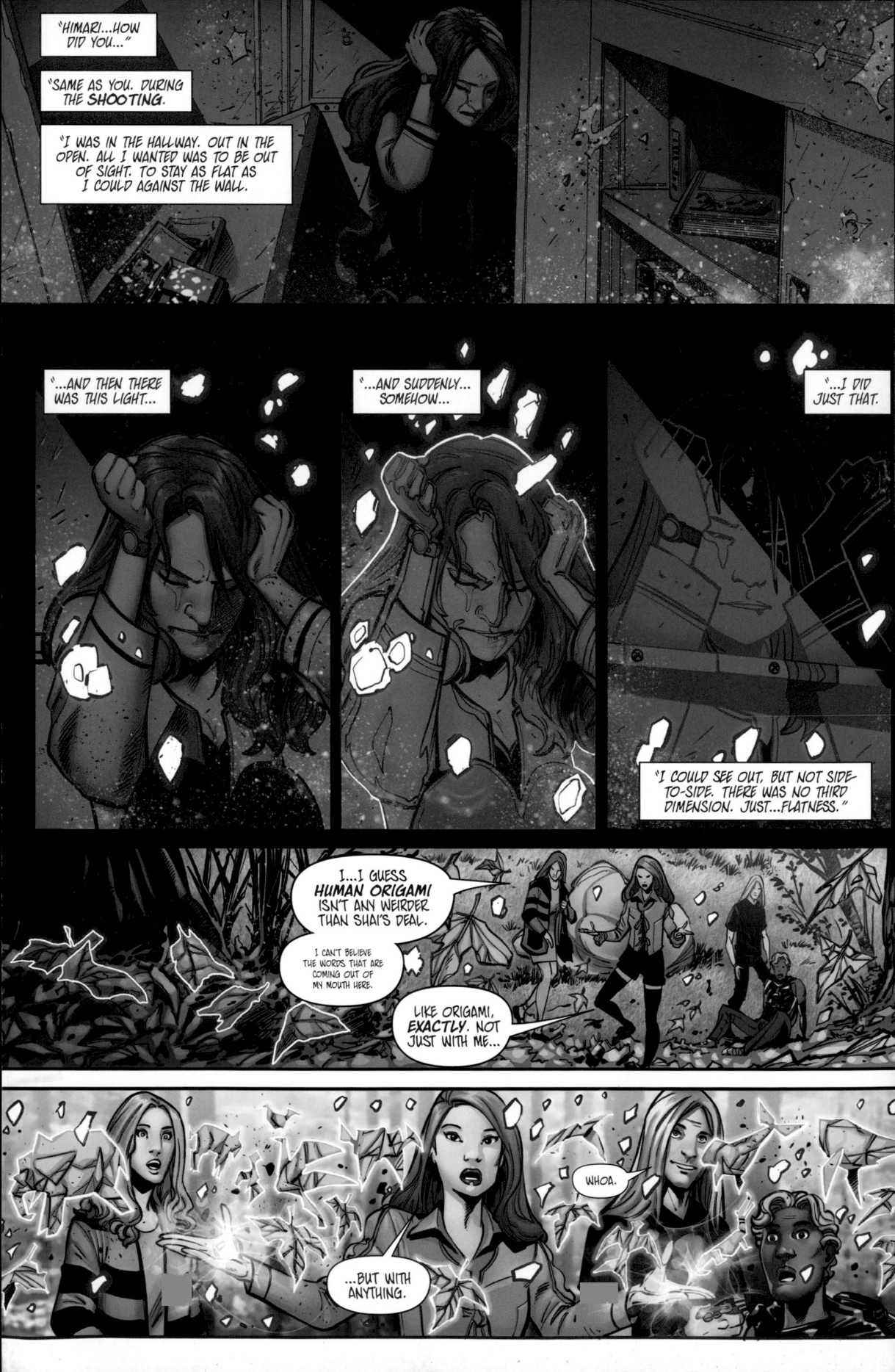

AAAAH!

YAAAAH!

'sup.

KARMAGRAM.

COOOOL.

BWAHHA HAHAHAHA

I LAUGH FOR WAY TOO LONG.

NOT JUST BECAUSE IT'S FUNNY.

BECAUSE IT'S THE FIRST TIME I'VE LAUGHED AT ALL SINCE MAY.

AND IT FEELS GREAT.

And say what? "I've turned... into an inhuman monster"?

But until I find some way to... to CONTROL this, I don't know what to SAY without freaking them out WORSE.

I miss them. I miss them so much. I hate that they're still LOOKING for me.

I WANT to tell 'em. BUT EVERY TIME I OPEN MY MOUTH, I JUST CAN'T. HIMARI. NOW YOU THREE. DR. ZHAO. BUT OTHER'N THAT--

--IT'S LIKE THE WORDS STICK IN ME THROAT, YEAH? I LOVE MY BROTHER LIKE NOTHIN' ELSE, BUT EVEN HE DOESN'T--

WAIT. YOU SAW DR. ZHAO, TOO? I DID TELL HER.

THE-- WHAT-DO-YOU-CALL-IT--

"--THE GRIEF COUNSELOR LADY. WHO ELSE HERE WENT TO HER? EVERYBODY?"

AND SHE'S THE ONLY ONE I TOLD ABOUT THE LIGHT AND THE...

ONLY ONE WE ALL TOLD ABOUT THIS... THE ONLY ONE.

WE ALL WENT TO HER, AND THEN NONE OF US WERE ABLE TO TELL OUR STORIES. HOLY FUCK.

WHAT THE FUCK DID SHE DO TO US?

WHAT NOW?
NOTHIN' NOW.
TOO LATE TO DO SOMETHIN' ON FRIDAY. COME MONDAY, THOUGH.
WE'RE CUTTIN' HOMEROOM.
AND WE ARE GONNA GO KNOCK ZHAO'S GADDAM DOOR DOWN.
WE'RE GONNA FIND OUT WHAT THE HELL'S HER STORY...
...AND WHO ELSE LIKE US SHE'S BEEN MESSIN' WIT..
WE CAN'T BE THE ONLY ONES THAT GOT LIT UP.

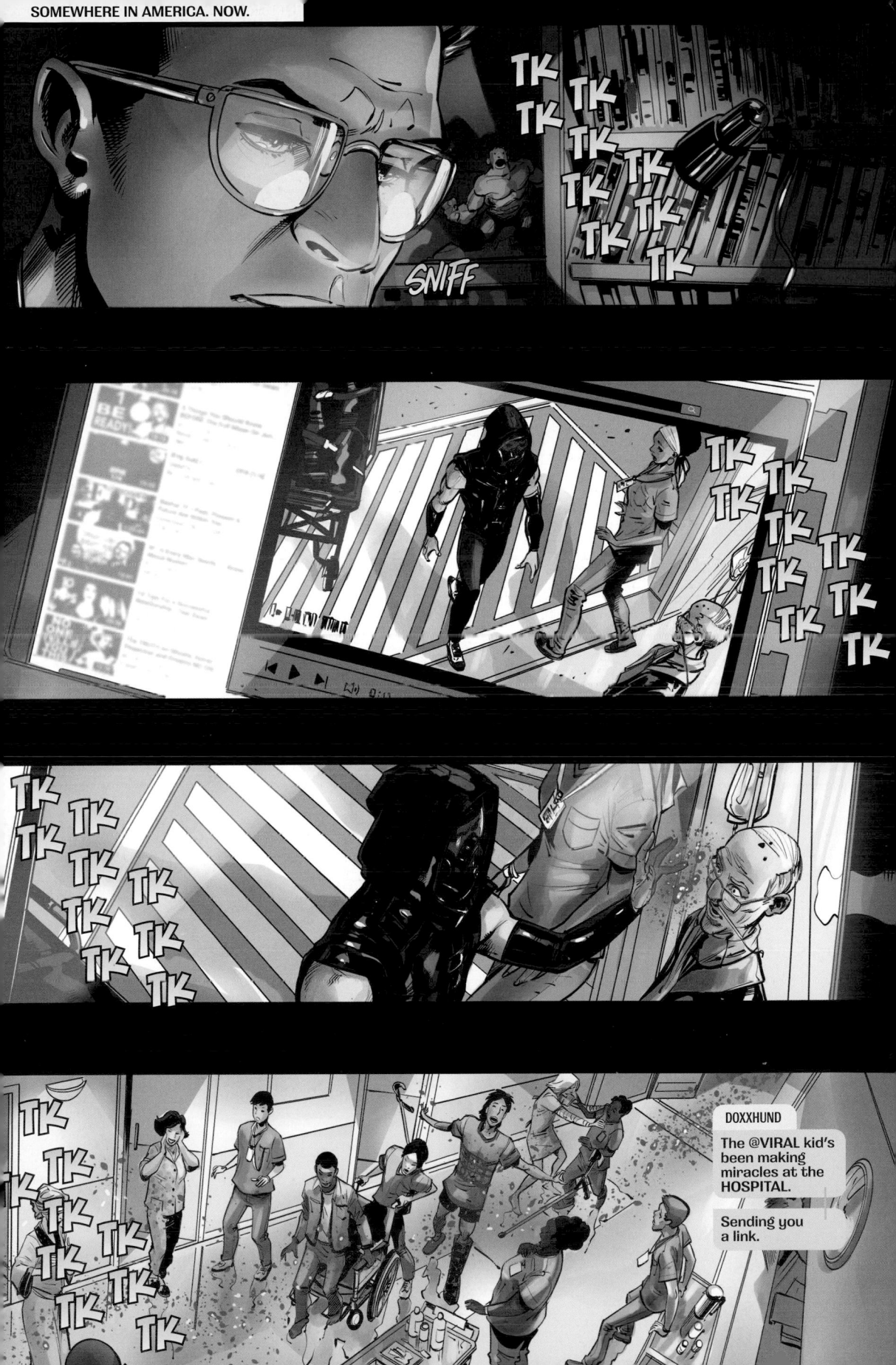

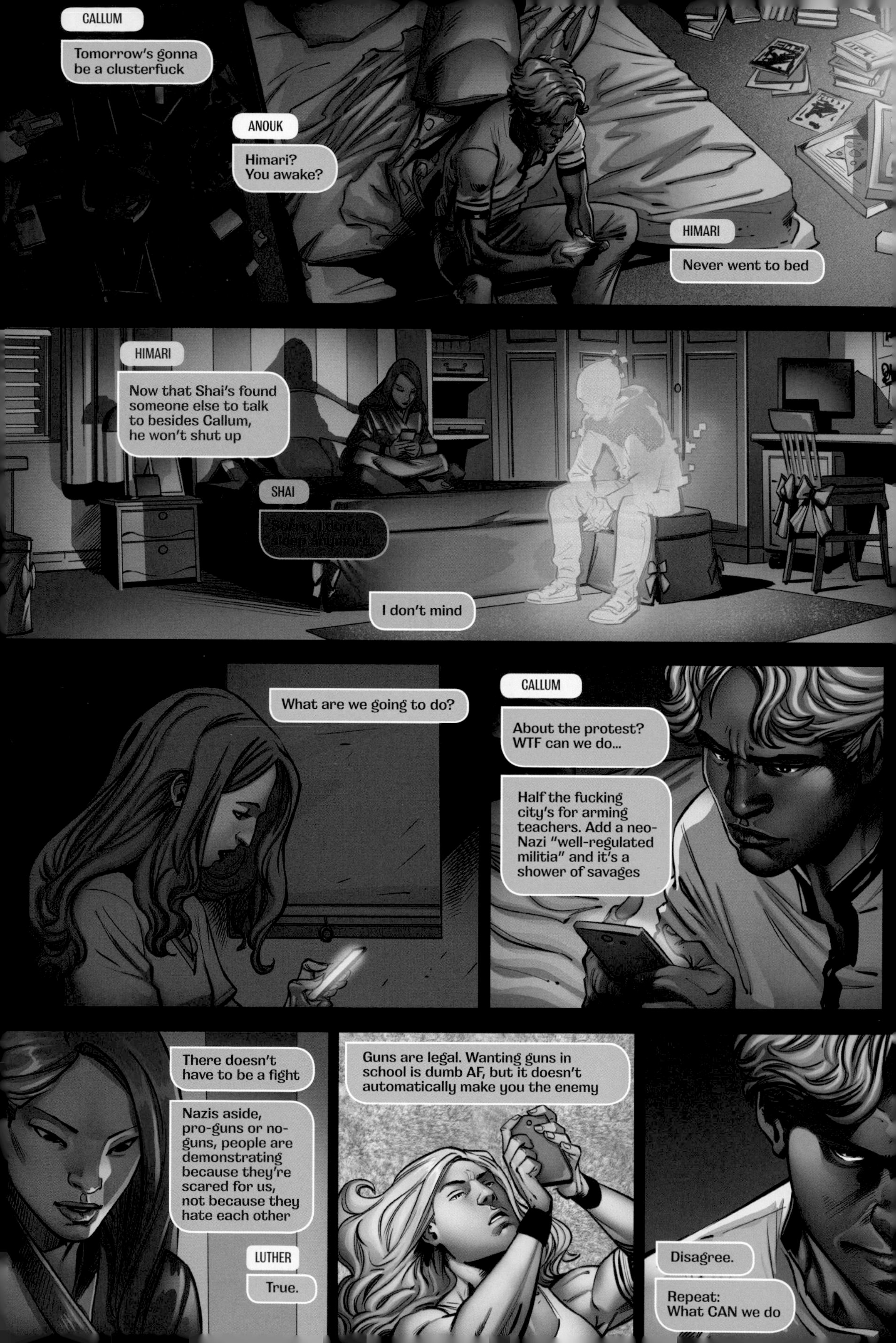

WHOA!
YOU OKAY?

I...I... I DON'T *KNOW*...

EVERYONE'S... EVERYONE'S *ANGRY*... *SCARED* AND *VERY ANGRY*...

...ONE GIRL... I THINK SHE SAW US IN THE *WOODS*...

WHAT'S EVERYONE LOOKING AT?

ODD.

"ODD"? SHE'S FECKING *GLOWING*.

ANOUK, ARE YOU OKAY?

I DON'T *KNOW*. I JUST GOT...*OVERRUN* BY...WHAT EVERYONE'S *FEELING*...

...ESPECIALLY THAT *MYSTERY GIRL*.

I...I DON'T KNOW. LOOK, I'M NOT SURE WHAT THE *PLAN* IS. MAYBE THERE'S ONLY A FEW ALT-RIGHT.

NOPE. MORE JUST SHOWED. THOSE ARE SOME PRETTY BIG *ROACH TAXIS*.

COUPLE OF **LEADERS** ARE HANGING BACK.

WE OUTNUMBER **THOSE** FUCKERS.

I SAY WE MAKE 'EM CALL THIS SHIT **OFF.**

ANOUK, YOU CAN'T **DEFEND** YOURSELF. STAY **BACK,** ALRIGHT?

NOT ALRIGHT. YOU KNOW WHAT CHANGED THE **MOST** AFTER THE SHOOTING?

I DON'T EVER WANT TO FEEL **HELPLESS** AGAIN.

DO YOU **READ?**

GROUP FOUR, CAN YOU HEAR ME? **HELLO?**

WALKIES NOT **WORKING?** YOU JUST CAUGHT THE **WAVE,** ASSHOLES.

REGIMENTS TWO AND **THREE! DEPLOY!**

FECK YE.

=HHUCKK-K-K=

MARTY? YOU **SICK,** DUDE?

OH, FECK...

...THERE'S MORE OF 'EM THAN WE THOUGHT...

IS HE BEING **GASSED?** HE'S BEING **GASSED!**

WHAT THE **HELL?**

THIS AIN'T HALLOWEEN, PUNKASSES.

--THE **FUCK**--?

SOMETHING'S HAPPENING NEAR THE **BUSES**! LET'S **GO**!

LOOKS LIKE A **FIGHT'S** BROKEN OUT!

DERRINGTON! HUMPHRIES! GET **ON** IT!

GREAT. REPORTERS **AND** COPS.

I WAS AN IDIOT TO THINK WE COULD STOP THIS.

WHAT DO I **DO**? I KNOW WHAT MY **GUT** IS TELLING ME.

THERE'S SOME **REASON** TO KEEP **FOCUSING** ON THAT GIRL.

FIND HER.

BACK OFF, MAN.

I CAN DO THIS ALL DAY.

CAMERAS. FORGOT ABOUT THAT. MASK'S AREN'T EVERYTHING. IF THEY CATCH TOO MUCH OF US, WE'RE SCREWED.

WHATEVER WE'RE SUPPOSED TO DO WITH THESE POWERS, IT'S A WRAP IF WE GET OUTED.

GOOD THING WE HAVE SHAI ON THE TEAM.

'SCUSE ME...

'SCUSE ME...

ANTIFA, RIGHT? FIGURES. SCUM.

YOU SOYBOYS NEED TO *LEARN* THAT AN *ARMED SCHOOL* IS A *SAFE SCHOOL.* WE WON'T LET YOU PUSH YOUR *PUSSY AGENDA.*

HERE'S MY "AGENDA," YE CUNTS.

AAAAAAHH--!

YOU! YOU WERE IN THE *WOODS* YESTERDAY! ARE YOU *WATCHING* US? WHO--

DON'T TOUCH ME!

≡UNNFFF≡

"LISTEN TO ME!

"YOU GOT THE POWER, *TOO.* I DON'T KNOW WHO YOU ARE OR WHAT YOU CAN *DO...*"

...BUT THERE *MUST* BE A *REASON* I'M *DRAWN* TO YOU, SAME AS I WAS *CALLU--*

--SAME AS I WAS WITH *VIRAL* AND THE *OTHERS!* IT'S YOUR *POWER!* I DON'T KNOW WHAT IT *IS,* OR HOW *ANY* OF THIS IS *HAPPENING...*

...BUT IF YOU CAN, HELP BREAK THIS *UP,* BEFORE SOMEBODY GETS *KILLED.*

LET 'EM. PEOPLE *SUCK.*

PLEASE.

DON'T EVEN DO IT *FOR* THEM, THEN! THERE ARE *LITERAL NAZIS HERE!* YOU DON'T THINK THEY'LL COME AFTER *YOU* NEXT?

YOU'VE GOT *SO MUCH RAGE* INSIDE YOU THAT IT PHYSICALLY *HURTS!* I CAN *TELL!* IF YOU KEEP HOLDING IT *IN,* IT'LL EAT YOU *ALIVE!*

LET IT *OUT.*

HOLY SHIT.

JESUS--!

HE AIN'T TAKIN' YOUR CALLS, FUCKWIT.

MASHUP! PAPERDOLL! LET'S MOVE! WAVE, ORDER THESE FUCKERS AWAY!

GET OUT. NOW.

YOU SAW WHAT HAPPENED WHEN I GOT INSIDE THOSE CAMERAS?

WANNA SEE WHAT HAPPENS WHEN I GET INSIDE YOUR BRAINS?

...UHHHH...

LET'S GO! LET'S GO! LET THESE IDIOTS DESTROY THEMSELVES! FUCK THEIR KIDS!

LET THE BLOOD BE ON THEIR HANDS!

WHAT'S YOUR *NAME*? WHAT DO WE *CALL* YOU?

THAT WAS *AMAZEBALLS*. YOU'RE LIKE *US*!

HOW DID YOU--

LEAVE

ME

ALONE!

ANOUK, WAS THAT *YOU* WHO DID THAT? IS THAT YOUR *POWER?* YOU SAVED OUR *ASSES*!

WASN'T ME. TELL YOU LATER.

LET'S... LET'S JUST GET *OUT* OF HERE BEFORE WE'RE *FOUND*, OKAY...?

HUMANITY FIRST

School shootings like the one that inspired our story happen in real life in this country with despicable frequency. We've reached out to various students who have survived these shootings and have invited them to speak their minds openly in the pages of IGNITED, saying whatever they feel needs saying.

10.01.15

Kindra Neely is a survivor of the Umpqua Community College shooting in 2015. She uses art to inspire connection and understanding and hopes to make children's comics in the future.

Much of the narrative surrounding mass shootings is focused on the shooter's motivation. We ask ourselves and each other, "Why did they do it? What makes a person enter a room of unsuspecting strangers and open fire? What led them to do that?" We analyze and dig for stories about mistreatment and abuse. We accept a narrative that isn't true, that they were outcasts and unloved, because that lie is an easier pill to swallow than the truth.

Nothing made them do it. Their actions seem senseless because they are senseless. We, as a nation, have to accept that in order to move on. Instead of focusing on the *why*, we need to focus on the *how*. How do we prevent this in the future? How do we help those who have already suffered? Not a second more should be spent focusing on the shooters. They are not affected by what they have done. We are.

It is time we take the narrative back. Let our grief and our strength be the rally cry for change. Let our stories unite us through empathy and compassion. No more silence. No more fear. Just us, and the tenacity to make tomorrow better than yesterday.

–Kindra Neely
May 2019

03.05.01

On March 5, 2001, Rachel Maurice was a junior at the Santana High School shooting in Santee, CA. Two students ages 14 and 17 were killed and 13 others including an unarmed school resource officer were shot multiple times but survived.

As a survivor, the hardest times in my life were when I felt alone in my brokenness. Suicide is a risk that is rising exponentially among mass tragedy survivors. I have PTSD, and it was a very difficult process to find a trauma therapist. Once I did, the high cost makes it at times unattainable when I need the help the most. If you feel the same, call or text the National Suicide Prevention Hotline at 800-273-8255 (TALK).

The discussion should not be about gun rights or gun laws. There is not a law in the books that would have saved my friend Randy and classmate Bryan that day. The focus should be on the mental health provided to survivors of gun violence. Survivors are all too often left shattered and alone to pick up the pieces. Without the right help, many of us cannot find the way out of our brokenness. If you are a survivor, please know there is an army of others that know your pain. Together, we can overcome the evil that tried to break us.

–Rachel Maurice
June 2019

MEET THE IGNITED

CALLUM HEALY

Codename: @viral
Age: 17
Goal: To course-correct what he sees as unjust social problems and corrupt governments.

Ignition phase and ability:
During the school shooting, one of his only friends is wounded and for the first time in his life, Cal shows something other than disdain. While trying to hide from the attacker, Cal is shot, igniting an ability to control all types of micro-organisms, diseases, and viruses—not limited to those in the human body.

HIMARI SAITO

Codename: @paperdoll
Age: 16
Goal: To help make the world less dark; to show people a better way to live than simply as cogs in dreary corporate jobs; and to summon her own courage when dealing with her father.

Ignition phase and ability:
When the shooting occurs, Himari has nowhere to hide. Igniting under the stress, she becomes two-dimensional, all but disappearing in the environment. She can move through space unseen, sliding across surfaces and through cracks. She will soon discover that she can flatten objects as well and mentally fold them into intricate origami sculptures that she can control.

LUTHER RAY HENSCHEN

Codename: @mashup
Age: 18
Goal: To have fun so long as he doesn't hurt anyone in the process. Luther Ray tries to find acceptance by making sure that no one else feels left out.

Ignition phase and ability:
Luther is hanging out with the school drumline, trying to convince them to incorporate a metal beat, when the shooter strikes. Luther, not realizing he's been hit, ignites, enabling him to grab whatever materials are around him and meld them into a makeshift shield. Luther learns that he can merge inorganic objects together. Though delighted by this ability, Luther decides to keep it a secret from his very conservative family.

SHAI FAREDA HADANE

Codename: @wave
Age: 16
Goal: To use his abilities to help his friends spread their message across the globe. Shai longs to find a way to get back into his physical body.

Ignition phase and ability:
He's in the school radio station when the shooting begins and is one of the first to be shot—strategically, so that he can't get the word out. As he lies dying, he thinks about all the things he hasn't said in his life and suddenly ignites. Transforming, Shai finds himself lost in the electromagnetic spectrum, appearing on TV screens, phones and radio broadcasts, asking if anyone can hear him. Now, existing as a noncorporeal waveform, Shai has the ability to manipulate light, vibrations, and electromagnetism. He's able to manipulate any electronic device within range and can use antennae and satellites to boost his signals. He can also control visible light to generate realistic holograms and, with effort, move most objects with any trace of metal in them.

ANOUK LOVARI

Age: 17
Goal: To help make society more honest and safe for people to live in, and to find belonging and purpose in a world that seems damaged. Anouk quickly emerges as the team's reluctant leader, the glue that holds them together.

Ignition phase and ability:
During the shooting, the students nearest Anouk begin following her lead and moving in unison—almost as one entity—providing care for the injured. They find themselves organizing around her, hanging on her every word. Anouk, who doesn't yet realize she has ignited, can alchemize emotions, tapping into people's feelings (including her own), mix-matching and transferring them to others. She can't create emotions or project her own, but she can unite others in empathy.

MARISOL FLORES

Codename: @terror
Age: 16
Goal: To protect her family from retaliation after she leaves the gang she was affiliated with.

Ignition phase and ability:
Marisol longs to push others away and keep them at arm's length. Now, with her ignited powers, she can deflect everything within her radius—earth, trees, people—with an energy that warps objects in ways that would make even a physicist's head explode.

IGNITED

COVER GALLERY

A: This IGNITED#1 variant cover, drawn by Phil Briones and colored by Lee Loughridge, was offered exclusively to American retailers during the Diamond Retailer Summit that took place in May 2019.

B: Brought to life by John Cassaday and Paul Mounts, this is the Shai-centric variant cover to IGNITED#2. A collector's item!

C: Another John Cassaday gem, this Himari/Paperdoll cover was sold as a rare 2019 San Diego Comic Con Exclusive. Laura Martin added her fantastic colors to it.